"Artie?" He kept his voice quiet. "Do you think you've seen or done anything I haven't?"

Her head jerked up at that. In the glow of the firelight he saw her face pale.

"Something got you put on leave," he said. "I heard the call. Leave with pay. That usually means a terrible event. That you were involved in violence. Am I right?"

She rose from her recliner and began pacing. "I don't want to think about it."

He nodded, leaning back, making himself as unthreatening as he could. "I can sure understand that."

"So you talk about it?" she demanded, turning on him.

"I just did."

"How can you talk about it without thinking about it?"

"You can't." He waited, knowing she might not speak another word to him but determined not to press her any further.

CONARD COUNTY: KILLER IN THE STORM

New York Times Bestselling Author
RACHEL LEE

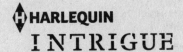

Conard County: Killer in the Storm deals with topics that some readers may find difficult, including rape, sexual assault and domestic violence.

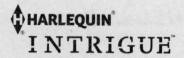

HARLEQUIN®
INTRIGUE™

Recycling programs for this product may not exist in your area.

ISBN-13: 978-1-335-59126-5

Conard County: Killer in the Storm

Copyright © 2023 by Susan Civil-Brown

For questions and comments about the quality of this book, please contact us at CustomerService@Harlequin.com.

Harlequin Enterprises ULC
22 Adelaide St. West, 41st Floor
Toronto, Ontario M5H 4E3, Canada
www.Harlequin.com

Printed in U.S.A.

Rachel Lee was hooked on writing by the age of twelve and practiced her craft as she moved from place to place all over the United States. This *New York Times* bestselling author now resides in Florida and has the joy of writing full-time.

Books by Rachel Lee

Harlequin Intrigue

Conard County: The Next Generation

Visit the Author Profile page at Harlequin.com.

CAST OF CHARACTERS

Artie (Artemis) Jackson—Deputy with Conard County Sheriff's Department. Has nightmares over a recent domestic violence case she had to intervene in.

Boyd Connor—Retired army veteran on a hike from the East Coast to the West Coast while waiting for permission to see his daughter. The hike helps him deal with his rage and sense of failure over his daughter.

Herman Jackson—Artie's father. He has early-onset Alzheimer's disease, which distresses him as much as Artie.

Linda Connor—Boyd's daughter, sixteen. Victim of rape, still raw, doesn't want to see her estranged father.

Shelley Connor—Boyd's ex-wife, who is trying to prevent him from seeing Linda.

Billy Lauer—Arrested by Artie when he brutally tried to kill his wife.

Willie and Joe Lathrop—They want to kill Artie rather than let her testify against their friend Billie Lauer.

Chapter One

Sheriff's Deputy Artie Jackson's headlights picked out the man with a backpack. He strode beside the desolate, dark highway in Conard County, Wyoming.

She didn't want to stop, but she did.

She'd just come from the most brutal domestic violence scene she'd ever witnessed. The bleeding woman lying beneath the beast who was trying to strangle her. The man refusing to listen to Artie Jackson. Ignoring the gun she threatened him with.

Reaching for her baton and beating the man with it repeatedly, feeling flesh and maybe bone crushing beneath it.

The moment when he'd reared up and come at her, ignoring her baton and pummeling her. Backup arriving just in time. Stumbling outside and vomiting until she had only dry heaves to give, dry heaves that wouldn't quit. The medevac chopper arriving to take the woman, still barely alive.

The struggling, yelling monster handcuffed and needing three deputies to wrestle him into the SUV cage.

The paramedic offering her help that she refused. Giving a brief official statement to another deputy.

She knew she'd done the right thing, but now she'd have to recover from it and live with it.

Ten miles down the road her stomach still roiled, her body shook, her mind refused to let go of the images, the sensations of that baton striking. She hardly noticed her own bruises.

Now there was a man walking along the dark roadside. God, she wanted to drive by, to leave him to deal with his own mess, to just get herself home. To warm herself, drink some brandy, try to forget.

The last thing she wanted to deal with was another man. Any man.

But the night, the approaching blizzard, wouldn't allow her to ignore him.

She flipped on her roof lights, blared her horn just once. He stopped walking and faced her as she approached. She rolled down the window on the passenger side.

"Get in," she said, her voice flat, revealing nothing of her inner turmoil.

"Why?" he asked, calmly enough. "I haven't done anything."

"Damn it!" she said, her frustration and anger erupting. "It's starting to sleet. A bad storm is moving in. You'll freeze to death if you don't get shelter. Now get in. I'll take you to the motel in town."

So close to home, but now delayed by a fool who didn't have the sense to take care of himself.

"I'm fine," he answered, still calm.

"Like hell you are. Get in or I'll call for backup. Out here we don't drive past people who might freeze to death from exposure."

He looked away briefly, then returned his attention to her. He was tall, his square face rugged. A dark watch cap tugged down over his ears. His eyes nearly invisible.

He spoke, his voice deep. "In the back?"

In the cage. She drew a deep breath, reaching for reason. "Passenger seat. You're not under arrest. Yet."

When she unlocked the doors, he threw his pack on the back seat. A huge backpack, maybe seventy pounds. Steel frame. The kind a hiker carried on a long trek.

Her mind still functioned clearly enough to take in even the small details. She clung to them.

As soon as he was safely belted in beside her, she hit the gas, wanting to hurry, knowing that her official vehicle would keep her from being stopped. Wondering if she should keep her flashers on.

But only a fool would be out driving right now. Conditions were getting dangerous. Those conditions applied to her, too.

For the first two miles, she said nothing. He sat quiet and motionless beside her.

"What are you doing out here?" she asked, as if she gave a damn, but it was a cop question and the cop inside her was still working.

"Walking," he answered.

"I could see that. Where are you going?"

"The next mile."

Well, that was no freaking answer at all. "Are you homeless?"

"No. I'm just walking across the country."

Beyond that, Artie didn't care. She didn't question why he would do such a thing. Merely a confirmation, perhaps, that he wasn't the smartest guy.

Or maybe he was on the run. She ought to check him out. But just then, with her sickened stomach twisted into a knot so hard it hurt like hell, she didn't care.

Get him to the motel. Drop him off with a warning. Deal with him in the morning.

She wanted that brandy. She wanted to build a fire in her fireplace and stare into it. She needed to check on her dad. Important things. More important than the jerk sitting beside her.

But when she pulled up at the La-Z-Rest motel, the only motel in town, the no-vacancy sign glowed in red neon. Well, yeah, she thought. With the storm coming in over the mountains, nobody was moving, from truckers to random tourists who were always heading anywhere but Conard City.

What was she supposed to do with the jerk sitting beside her? Throw him out? Drop him at the truck stop diner and tell him to drink coffee for the next four days?

For the second time that night, reality crashed in on her.

Gritting her teeth, she jammed her Suburban into gear. "You've got a choice, make it fast. I can put you in a holding cell at the sheriff's office. You won't be locked in, not that that'll help much. It stinks of too many drunks."

"And the other choice?"

"You can sleep on my couch. And no, I won't be alone with you. So decide."

"You don't want me at your place."

"Of course I don't," she snapped. "But those holding cells have been used for a century and even bleach can't clean out the stench. So I'm giving you a choice. Take it, one way or the other."

"I'm a stranger," he replied. "Are you sure you want me in your home?"

"I'm a cop. I have a baton, I have my service pistol and I have some tae kwon do. You step out of line and you'll get more trouble than you bargain for." As she'd learned of herself tonight.

"Your place," he said finally. "But just for the night."

Right, she thought. Well, maybe someone would leave the motel in the morning. Another fool who might cause some other deputy the kinds of nightmares that came from an auto accident scene.

"I'm Boyd Connor," he said.

"Artie Jackson." As if she cared what his name was.

Right then she felt the world was populated by jerks and monsters and she'd have been happy never to see another soul again.

Ten minutes later, she pulled into her own driveway. Lights poured from the windows, along with a flicker of the television screen. The sleet had begun to sting with the rising wind.

"Come on," she said.

The man followed her, backpack in hand. Into a space she'd called home her entire life. Shabby around the edges but clean. She was something of a clean freak, ordering as much of her world as she could.

Her dad sat in his recliner, intent on the TV. She wasn't reassured to find him watching a cartoon.

"Hi, Dad," she said, going to kiss his forehead. Beside him on the end table she saw a plate of food. "I see Clara brought you dinner. Was it good?"

"Fine," he answered with a vague smile. Then his gaze tracked to the man. "Who?" he asked.

The man dropped his backpack near the door. "I'm Boyd Connor, sir."

"Herman," her dad answered. "I'm Herman."

"Boyd's going to sleep on the sofa tonight," Artie told her father. "Bad blizzard."

"I saw the news." Then her dad returned his attention to the TV.

Artie headed for the safe in her bedroom where she stowed her pistol. She left her jacket lying on the bed. She wasn't worried about the Connor guy. She already knew what she could do with that damn baton, and she kept it with her. The gun was another matter. She didn't want her dad to ever get his hands on it.

Artie returned to the living room and looked at Boyd Connor, really taking him in for the first time. A strong, square face, darkened with several days' beard growth. Brown eyes. Dark hair, a little messy when he pulled off his watch cap. A powerful build with narrow hips, long legs. Taller than average. Her mind stored those details.

Artie picked up the dinner dishes, reaching for some normalcy. She pointed with her chin. "That's the sofa. It has a pull-out bed, but after all these years I can't guarantee it'll be comfortable."

"I'll be fine," Boyd Connor answered. "I appreciate the hospitality."

Civility reared its head even in the midst of her inner turmoil. "You must be hungry. I know I am. I've got some frozen dinners."

"Thanks. Whatever you have."

She turned again to her father. "You want anything, Dad? Still hungry? Maybe some milk or coffee?"

"I'm fine."

He was always fine, a situation that frustrated Artie because she needed to do more for him. But he didn't seem to want or need any more than the basics. God, she loved that man so much her heart ached with it. Her daddy. Slipping steadily away.

"Can I help?" Boyd asked.

She shook herself free of her endless, growing sorrow. "I'm just going to pop the meals in the microwave. I eat out of the containers, unless that's a problem for you."

For the first time he smiled, a faint smile but still a smile. "If you had any idea what I've been eating for years you wouldn't even ask."

Well, that sparked a dull interest, but she didn't pursue it. "After we eat I want to see your ID."

"I'd be surprised if you didn't."

She entered the same kitchen her mother had used, the same pots and pans and dishes. The dishwasher, her mother's pride so long ago, had died and Artie hadn't replaced it. Who needed a dishwasher for two people? She'd added a few things over the years. A small air fryer oven that served for baking or toasting for two. An induction coil for her dad to cook quickly on and safely. And the induction carafe to boil water. She didn't want her father to use the gas stove for any reason. In fact, she often thought about permanently turning off the gas supply to the stove.

She pulled three meals out of the freezer, two for Boyd. As big as he was, his appetite must be large. Basic frozen ziti. She also grabbed a box of frozen Texas garlic toast. Her dad liked that and it would toast quickly in the air fryer. Maybe he could be coaxed to eat a slice or two.

While she waited on the microwave and the coffee-pot, she looked around her at a room full of memories, good memories. The white-painted cabinets that had begun to dull with age. The ceramic tile countertops, also white, that her father had installed so many years ago. Artie's reluctance to change anything had good reasons. Emotional reasons, not only for herself but for her father, as well.

Focusing on happy memories was good. At least for a while. Her most recent memories needed to be buried in the deepest darkest hole she could find.

Except she knew they wouldn't be. One way or another she was going to have to wrap her mind around it all.

BOYD CONNOR HAD learned something about Artie Jackson in the brief time he had known her. She was forceful, prickly. Something bad had happened to her before she picked him up.

Then there was her father. Boyd didn't need a road map to see what was happening there. A huge grief for her. He was familiar with grief.

He dropped his backpack on the floor by the sofa and sat. Understandably, Artie hadn't wanted him in her kitchen. He was already encroaching enough and he didn't feel good about it. Maybe he should have chosen the holding cell after all.

She was a pretty woman with inky hair bobbed to her shoulders, and bright blue eyes. A heart-shaped face. And as she'd doffed her jacket he'd seen a good figure despite the gun belt around her hips. Other than the baton, the gun belt was gone now, a brave decision considering she'd invited a total stranger into her home. He felt a flicker of admiration for her.

The two of them ate at her dinette in the kitchen, served out of the containers as she'd warned him. In the living room, in front of the TV, Herman Jackson ate garlic toast and accepted a cup of coffee.

Conversation at the table was limited. Artie evidently had things she didn't want to discuss. Boyd had plenty of things he didn't even want to *think* about.

He let the silence continue, giving them both space. Casual conversation seemed out of place.

But still, he felt the need to make some minor connection since she'd picked him up like a lost dog on the roadside.

"How long is this weather going to last?"

"Until winter is over." Then she raised her head. "They're predicting maybe three days. Then it'll take time to thoroughly clear the mountain roads to make them safe for trucks. So I can't say for sure. You in a hurry?"

A hurry to continue his own self-imposed penance? He supposed he could do that as well here for a few days as anywhere. But it wouldn't help with his fury and despair. Walking had been helping that. He didn't answer her.

He cleaned up what little there was from their dinner. Then Artie said, "I need your ID."

"It's in my pack. I'll get it." Not that she would find out very much. He didn't exactly have a big profile out there on the internet. The invisible man. He preferred it that way, especially now.

She took his driver's license and passport, then retrieved a laptop to place it on the kitchen table. She checked once more on her father, then said, "You might as well make yourself comfortable on the couch. You can take a shower after I get mine. If you want."

It had been a couple of days since his last truck stop shower. He definitely wanted another one, but using her bathroom seemed like a huge trespass. She hadn't needed to offer it.

Interesting woman, conflicting urges. A clear need to be left alone while extending the courtesy of her home. For the first time in a long time, he felt interested in something outside himself, outside his own family.

ARTIE WAS FRUSTRATED. So much for coming home, lighting a fire and drinking brandy.

But she had to learn about the stranger in her home. Her father was vulnerable even if she wasn't.

She logged into her departmental account and started the wheels spinning on a background check. Then she hit the web, searching for anything she could find. Very little was hidden on the web. There *had* to be something.

She burrowed in deeper and deeper until finding a small blurb that had been put out there by someone who was following people who'd served in a certain paratrooper regiment.

Master Sergeant Boyd L. Connor. Retired Army with disability. Three tours in Afghanistan. Maybe that alone was enough to make a man walk alone so far from anywhere. If indeed he was walking far. Clearly avoiding human interaction.

Well, if he had a record of any kind, the background check would turn it up. She closed the laptop and returned to the living room to give Boyd his ID. And now, given his background, she felt a bit foolish for having told him she wasn't worried about him being in her house because she had her police equipment and tae kwon do. This guy probably exceeded her own experience with self-protection.

"Find anything?" he asked as he tucked his papers away.

"You're the invisible man."

Again a smile flitted across his face. "Hard to do these days."

"I'll have your background check sometime tomorrow."

Then she bent to light the fire already laid on the fireplace. She didn't ask Boyd if he minded. He sat on the couch, staying out of the way. Good.

Then she poured herself the long-awaited brandy and flopped on the second recliner. Cartoons still played on the TV. She didn't offer to give Boyd brandy, but eventually awareness of her own rudeness stirred her. "If you want some brandy, help yourself."

"I'm fine, thanks."

Another man who was *fine*. God, she was getting sick of that word.

The crackling fire cast a soothing glow through the room along with some dancing shadows. Between it and the brandy she began to uncoil. It wouldn't last, but she would take what she could get.

But now she felt her own bruises, becoming more painful as they spread. Ice, she should ice them. Hell, no. She didn't need the chill. The internal chill already felt bone deep. Ibuprofen. Later.

Eventually she saw that her dad was dozing. Smothering a sigh, she rose, trying not to wince. She went to him and touched his shoulder. His eyes opened.

"Dad, it's time to go to bed."

He nodded and closed the recliner, sitting up.

"You can take care of your teeth and pajamas, right?"

"Yeah. You know I can, for Pete's sake."

But she knew she'd have to check on him anyway. He could forget between one task and another. Not always. It wasn't that bad yet. But it was headed that way like a freight train rolling down the tracks.

"Teeth first," she reminded him. "Then pajamas."

"I *know* that," he snapped.

Another part of this disease she hated, the times he grew angry when reminded about his memory. The times he grew frustrated when he realized he couldn't remember. One stressor after another.

All of it worthwhile. This was the man who had cared for her when she was a child. Now the shoe was on the other foot and he deserved every bit of care she could provide.

She peeked in after he disappeared into the bathroom. His teeth were getting cleaned. Then she peeked in when he'd been in the bedroom for a while. He slept in his pajamas beneath a comforter. All was well. For a while.

She grabbed some ibuprofen from the medicine chest and, back in the living room, swallowed them with brandy. She kept trying to turn her thoughts away from earlier events. She knew beyond any shadow of a doubt that they were going to haunt her for a long time.

The phone rang, dragging her back into the middle of her mental and emotional mess. It was Gage Dalton, the sheriff.

"Hi, Artie," he said.

"Give me no bad news, Gage."

"It's not *bad* news. You know the regulations. Don't report for duty tomorrow. We have to put you on leave with pay until the psychologist clears you."

Everything inside Artie clenched. Weren't things already bad enough? "But, Gage, I need to work. I *need* to keep busy. I can do office work!"

"You know the rules," he repeated. "They're the same for everyone. You had a violent confrontation that left you physically battered."

"But how soon will I see a damn psychologist?"

"As fast as we can arrange it. I promise. In the meantime, look after yourself. And your father."

She disconnected without another word, becoming suddenly aware of Boyd's eyes on her.

"It must have been bad," was all he said.

"Bad enough," she answered shortly. "But I could still work."

He didn't answer for a moment, then said, "I know how bad it can get. Take the time. That's what I'm doing."

Which probably said a whole lot, she thought almost bitterly.

"Have another brandy. Kick back and relax as much as you can."

He had no right to advise her, but she didn't want the effort of telling him off.

"There doesn't seem to be anything else I can do." Then she flipped off the TV, sick to death of cartoons. Sick to death of what they meant about her father's mental state.

Sick to death of herself.

Chapter Two

Artie had gotten her shower; Boyd had followed her a few minutes later. At last, wrapped in her pajamas and a thick black robe, she settled on the second recliner with another snifter of brandy and put her feet up. Her baton remained close beside her, just in case. Outside the wind keened.

Boyd stretched out on the couch, wearing an old gray fleece sweat suit. She ought to get him a blanket. Hunt up a pillow. Well, he could ask if he wanted them. She was in no mood to wait on him.

Feet up on one arm at the end of the sofa, head pillowed on the other arm, he didn't look as if he could be terribly comfortable. Regardless, she heard him fall into the slow breathing of sleep.

Good for him. She wondered if she'd ever sleep again.

She didn't want to close her eyes. It was easier and safer to watch the flames dance. Not that it erased the images that had stamped themselves indelibly in her mind.

God! She didn't know what bothered her more, the

images of that man attacking his wife or the feeling of her baton landing on flesh with sickening thuds.

She'd become violent, maybe as violent as that beast. Justification didn't matter.

Violence. Her own violence. A part of her she'd never suspected existed to that degree.

Billy Lauer, having beaten his wife half to death, was trying to steal the last of her life with his hands around her throat. Wouldn't stop even when Artie shouted at him and waved her pistol.

A pistol she didn't dare shoot because he was so close to his wife. Because the bullet could have pierced walls and wounded or killed innocent people on the other side of them.

She'd had no choice, but that didn't make her feel better about herself. Not even a little bit.

Maybe Gage was right about her needing some time off, some time to work through this.

Because, sure as hell, she didn't know if she could trust herself to use necessary force again. Hesitation on her part could cost a life, a colleague's. Her own.

So it was more than internal self-loathing she had to deal with. She had to deal with trusting herself.

Slowly, despite everything, she fell into uneasy sleep. She didn't resist it. Tomorrow would come and all the problems would still be there.

Boyd woke during the night and saw Artie sleeping on the recliner. The orange glow of the fire danced over her face and he could tell she was sleeping restlessly. What the hell had happened to her?

Not that it was any of his business. Not that he should care. But the look on her face when she'd picked him up had told an ugly story of some kind.

Moving quietly, he went to the bathroom, then peeked out the curtains. The storm had reached full fury, making it almost impossible to see the house next door. In the distance he heard a struggling snow-plow, probably almost useless. Primary roads, though, had to be cleared as much as possible for emergencies, even if the task was thankless.

As much as he'd wanted to keep walking, he was grateful that Artie had given him shelter. He could have survived the elements—he'd done so before—but he was thankful he didn't need to.

In the kitchen, he filled a glass with water and sat at the dinette. He didn't sleep well as a rule. Nightmares followed him even into the deepest sleep, rousing him with either panic or fury. Or despair.

He stared at the kitchen window, which gave him a view of the storm's anger, and recognized himself in that wild fury. Because that's what part of him had become. Guilt heaped itself on top of the anger, and his own failure crowned the entire mess. Somewhere inside was a heart that wouldn't stop breaking. It was a freaking wonder that he could still breathe.

Purpose alone kept him moving. He had to get to his daughter. If she'd even see him.

But that was another thing he tried not to think about even though it plagued him constantly.

Briefly, the storm lessened. Flakes glittering in the

light through the kitchen window grew larger, gentler, as they feathered their way to the ground.

Maybe he wouldn't be trapped here much longer. Except that all too soon the ferocity returned. Nature venting herself on the world. Teaching lessons about the insignificance of man and animal.

He tried to focus his attention on the problems this storm would cause ranchers or people trying to travel. Like the truckers, always on a tight schedule.

It didn't help. His concern for people had been ripped away a while ago. Recent events had only hardened the disgust he felt. Not only with them but with himself.

Then there was the cop sleeping in the next room. Whatever had upset her so much that her boss wanted her to see a psychologist hadn't prevented her from stopping to pick him up to save him from the weather. A good soul, whatever she might be feeling. Prickly, angry, but good.

Her father. A man clearly suffering from dementia or Alzheimer's. A man she looked after despite everything else on her plate. A man she deeply loved. That had been apparent even in such a short time, even when Herman snapped at her.

Hard to deal with. Devastating for her. Boyd wondered how bad it had gotten for the two of them.

Then he heard the TV switch on. Rising, he went to look and saw that Herman had returned to his recliner. A weather channel occupied the screen. He hoped it didn't wake Artie.

Herman sat in his recliner, wearing his light blue

pajamas and slippers. He didn't look like an old man, rather appeared as if he were in his midsixties. Unshaven face, but he was still good-looking even if his face was lined with age. A thick shock of gray hair. He might have appealed to women of almost any age.

But Boyd was concerned about the TV waking Artie. As restless as she had been, she wasn't getting very good sleep and she needed every decent minute she could find.

He had an idea. Entering the room quietly, he walked around until he could squat facing Herman.

"Herman," he said quietly.

The man looked at him.

"Artie's sleeping. Why don't you come to the kitchen with me and we'll have some cocoa or something. How's that sound?"

"Boyd." Herman's eyes suddenly brightened with full intelligence. He looked toward Artie. At once he clicked the TV off. Then he eyed Boyd.

"Cocoa sounds good."

"Let's go, then."

Herman closed the recliner and followed Boyd into the kitchen where he sat at the table.

Boyd spoke. "Where do I find the stuff to make the cocoa?"

"Artie uses the packets. In the pantry. I'll get them."

Boyd waited while Herman rose and opened the large pantry. He emerged a half minute later with a box of instant cocoa packets.

"I'll make it," Herman said.

So Boyd sat at the table, watching. Herman filled the

induction carafe that fit on its own coil and started it boiling. Coffee mugs. Packets opened and emptied into the mugs. Herman might have forgotten some things, but he hadn't forgotten this.

Soon enough they sat across the table with hot mugs of cocoa before them. Boyd stirred his absently, wondering what he could talk to Herman about, needing to fill this man's silence with something positive.

"Artie worries about me too much," Herman said eventually. "I'm losing some of my memory, but I'm not that bad yet."

"I see that. So your memory? You're aware of it?"

"Sometimes. I can remember the past all right. It's stuff that happened a few days ago that gives me trouble."

Boyd nodded and sipped cocoa. "That must be tough."

Herman shrugged. "What you can't remember doesn't hurt you. But sometimes I forget important stuff."

That would probably bother Artie more than anything, Boyd thought. "Artie mentioned Clara. Is she your friend?"

Herman sipped more cocoa, then nodded. "We been friends for a long, long time. Always lived next door to each other. She's a widow. Like me."

Boyd drained his mug, then said, "So Clara brought you dinner tonight?"

"Yep. She does that when Artie has to work. Or we have dinner together. And sometimes all three of us eat together."

"That sounds nice."

Herman smiled. "Better than nice. Clara's a lot of fun. Got two good grandkids, too. Good boys."

Grandkids. Clearly Herman didn't have any, and Boyd wondered if that weighed on him. "Do you want grandkids, too?"

Herman shrugged. "Artie don't have time right now. Too much with her job and me."

"I don't think she feels you're a job."

Herman's smile faded. "Maybe not. But I still make work for her. Not too much yet, I don't think."

Boyd had no answer for that. How could he? But he was starting to feel sorry for this man who was fading mentally and knew it. A man who seemed to feel that he was becoming a burden on his daughter.

The wall clock over the sink said dawn was approaching, although with this weather Boyd didn't think they'd get much light for hours yet.

"Some storm," Herman remarked. "We get a bad one or two every winter, but usually it's okay. When the snow is dry, it blows for days, though. Big drifts from only a little snow."

At that moment, Artie entered the kitchen, yawning and rubbing her eyes. "You guys having a party without me?"

"Might could be," her father answered with a broad smile. "Want some cocoa?"

"Thanks, Dad, but I really want coffee. Lots and lots of coffee."

"That's my Artie. Just like her mom."

Artie hesitated, but only for an instant. A hesitation so slight that eyes other than Boyd's might have missed it. Was she still pained by the loss of her mother? Or was it something else?

His gaze followed her as she yawned again and made coffee. While the pot hissed and burbled, she leaned back against the counter, folding her arms.

Herman spoke. "Tell me you don't have to go out in this storm."

One corner of Artie's mouth lifted. "Not today, Dad."

"Then I don't have to worry." Herman looked at his mug. "Guess I want more cocoa."

"I'll make it," she answered. "I'm just standing around waiting on the coffee. You ever think about how much time we stand around waiting?"

"Never did," Herman answered.

"There's different kinds of waiting," Boyd answered. Like waiting for his daughter to be willing to see him. "Sometimes waiting is all you can do."

Artie nodded and filled the glass carafe again. The box of cocoa still stood on the counter where Herman had left it. "You want some cocoa, too, Boyd?"

"Sounds good, if you don't mind."

Her response was dry. "It is *ever* so much more work to make a second cup. I mean, I'll have to tear open another packet."

That brought a chuckle out of Herman, and Boyd saw Artie's face brighten at the sound. The love between the two was palpable.

Herman spoke. "It'll kill you, won't it?"

"Just about," Artie answered as she took the mugs

to the counter with her and emptied packets into them. The induction carafe heated the water in about the time it took the coffee maker to finish brewing.

"Looks wicked out there," she remarked as she brought the cocoa and coffee to the table. She joined them, sitting slightly closer to her father than to Boyd. Hardly surprising. What *was* surprising was that she was being so courteous to him, especially since she probably wanted him hanging around about as much as she wanted a wood sliver under a fingernail.

He was well and truly stuck here, however. After the way she had picked him off the roadside, he suspected that if he tried to leave now that baton of hers might bar his way. Or she might call for backup as she had threatened to last night.

The memory brought an almost-smile to his face. To muscles that had forgotten how to smile. Muscles that had become as frozen as the world outside.

Artie spoke. "How's Clara doing, Dad? I haven't seen her in a few days."

"She's fine," Herman answered.

"Always fine," Artie murmured, her gaze drifting away. Then she appeared to shake herself. "I'll check on her later. Make sure she's all set for this weather."

Herman turned his head. "You *know* she's ready for this, Artie. Lived here all her life."

Artie sighed. "I'm sure you're right, but neighbors check on neighbors, don't they?"

Herman nodded. "Always."

"Right. And it's your fault for teaching me that."

Herman laughed. "Okay, okay. Guess I taught you some things right."

"More than a few. Like you told me once, it was your job to get me to the age of eighteen alive."

Herman snorted. "I said that?"

"You know you did. And look at me. I'm nearly thirty and I'm still alive, so you did good."

"Never got the risk taker out of you, though."

Artie tilted her head. "Did you really want to?"

"Hell, no. Like your granddad used to say, *Kids are born with personalities. All you can do is dent them a little to get them in shape.*"

"I remember that," she replied. "Except the only denting you ever did to me was to raise your voice. Right through the roof."

"Got your attention, didn't I?" Herman's smile remained. "I never wanted to change you, girl. Just screw your head on a little tighter."

Father and daughter exchanged looks that once again broadcast a deep mutual love.

Boyd shifted slightly, knowing he was an intruder. But where could he go? He also hated the feeling that he was like a kid outside a candy store window, unable to experience the warmth of this kind of family. Knowing he never really had.

Herman fell silent, drifting away a bit. Artie frowned faintly when he said, "I think I'll go watch my shows now."

Then, without another word, he rose from the table. Artie watched him go, sorrow slipping across her face.

Boyd, perfectly aware he didn't have the right, asked anyway, "How bad is it?"

Her blue eyes sharpened as she looked at him. "What concern of yours is it?"

"Only that it's in front of me." That was all he could say when she had every right to resent his prying.

After a few beats, she rose and poured herself more coffee. "It's episodic," she answered finally. "For a long time I wasn't even sure it was more than ordinary forgetfulness. Apparently it is."

"Hard on you both."

"Goes without saying." She resumed her seat at the dinette but didn't look at him. She had gone to some dark place inside herself. There wasn't a damn thing he could do about that.

From the living room came the sound of voices. A weather program maybe? It didn't sound like cartoons.

Artie closed her eyes and Boyd suspected that in those voices she heard the future she couldn't prevent.

Life sucks, he thought. The question was whether it ever stopped sucking.

Chapter Three

Eventually gray light appeared, but the storm continued angrily. Artie checked the clock, then picked up her phone and stood looking out the front window while she called Clara.

"Hey, Clara, it's Artie. Thanks for bringing Dad his dinner last night."

Clara's warm voice answered her. "Never a problem, Artie. You know that. That old man and I have some good times together. Does he need me today?"

"I'll be here all day. Mainly I called to see if you were okay for the storm or if you wanted to come over here."

Clara laughed. "I'm okay. I always make sure I have plenty of stores on hand. I'm all bundled up in my fleece, looking at a nice fire. You need anything?"

"We're all set." Artie hesitated. "Do you want to spend the day here?"

Herman surfaced from the TV long enough to say, "Where you gonna put her, Artie, with Boyd here?"

Artie closed her eyes. *Oh, Dad.*

"I can leave," Boyd said quietly.

"Don't even think about it," Artie snapped. "I didn't rescue your butt to watch you leave and freeze it off!"

A long pause. Then Clara asked tentatively, "Is something wrong? What is Herman talking about?"

Artie drew a deep breath. This was going to sound stupid, she thought, but there it was. "I rescued a hiker alongside the road last night. The motel is full so he's here."

Artie could almost hear Clara chewing her lip. Finally the woman spoke. "Is that wise?"

"Was there a choice?"

"I guess not. Just as long as you and Herman are safe."

"We are," Artie answered with more confidence that she actually felt. She still didn't know diddly about Boyd Connor except he'd been in the Army. Thus far, however, he seemed harmless. "Anyway, I called about *you*."

"I'm really okay. I have my books, my fire and my food."

"You'll let me know, though? If you need anything?"

"Hell, yes. And the same goes for you and Herman. Call me every now and then, though. Put my mind at ease."

Artie agreed and disconnected. Then she turned to face the two men. Herman on his recliner, Boyd perched on the couch. The small house suddenly felt crowded.

"I guess I should make breakfast," she said. "We've all got to be hungry."

Boyd rose at once. "Tell me what you want. I'll do the cooking."

Artie looked at him. "You cook?"

One corner of his mouth lifted. "I can clean to white-glove standards, too. Just point me."

Despite herself, Artie felt amused. "Where'd you learn all that?"

His faced shadowed. "Once upon a time I took basic training. Once upon a time I had a family."

Then he rose and headed for the kitchen. "What's the menu?"

Artie stared after him. Once upon a time he'd had a family? She had the distinct feeling that that wasn't a happy story at all.

Nor did she want to hear it. Strangers passing like ships in the night. No involvement needed.

Besides, right now she didn't want to get involved with anyone or anything. She had a serious mental mess of her own she had to find a way to climb out of.

Like quicksand, the memories of yesterday kept pulling her down.

Herman spoke, his gaze still trained on the TV. "I told you Clara was fine."

Yes, he had. Just like he was always *fine*. She sometimes wondered how often her dad meant that, and how often he said it just to soothe her.

She supposed she'd never know.

WHILE COOKING WAS not Boyd's favorite thing, he was glad to be doing it. An unwanted guest in this house, he needed to do more than take up a couch and eat the Jacksons' food. He sure as hell didn't want to be waited on.

Artie pointed out the bacon, eggs, bread. Asked if he knew how to use the air fryer for toast and ran him through a brief lesson. Then she vanished, saying she needed to dress.

Boyd let go of the slight tension that had troubled him since he'd been forced into this woman's life. *Force* was a good word for it, too. He didn't doubt she would have called for backup if he'd refused to come with her last night. Not a doubt in the world. She seemed to have a backbone of steel.

Not that she'd been wrong to insist he come with her. She couldn't know that he'd survived similar conditions in the past. He would have made it through, however uncomfortably.

But being comfortable wasn't part of his life. Not during much of his past, and certainly not now.

He thought of his daughter, Linda, and his heart squeezed until it hurt. He deserved her feelings about him, but Linda didn't deserve what had happened to her. Then fury began to replace pain. The urge to kill had never been personal for him in the past, but it was now. He wanted to kill those who had raped his daughter.

Get a grip. Make breakfast. Be useful to someone.

It was an easy breakfast. A good thing, because he was no chef. But it *was* a meal he'd made for himself plenty of times in the past, and more recently since leaving the Army. He'd always believed that bacon topped the list of comfort foods.

Although comfort had left him in the dust, even with food.

While the bacon was sizzling on the frying pan, he poked his head into the living room. "How do you guys want your eggs?"

"Scrambled," Herman answered promptly. "Artie, too. Sometimes she puts cheese in them."

Cheese? Boyd went back to look in the fridge and found a bag of shredded cheddar. That would do.

He turned the bacon and cracked eggs into a chipped stoneware bowl. Two apiece plus one for the pot as they said. Then he shook his head and threw in a couple of extra eggs. He'd finish any leftovers. All that walking had given him the appetite of a stevedore.

Of course, that might mean he would leave Artie and Herman short on food. He shook his head, sighed and continued. If necessary he could hike through these conditions to the grocery.

He knew his own abilities and limits intimately. He'd had plenty of opportunities to learn.

He was on the second load of bacon, the whipped eggs waiting for their turn. He needed to start making the toast with the loaf of rye Artie had put out. The butter was on a plate nearby. Utensils and dishes easy to find. Another pot of coffee brewing. At least he hadn't forgotten how to time everything.

Artie appeared, wearing jeans, a blue fleece pullover and warm-looking slippers. "How's it going, Boyd?"

"For once everything is going according to plan. But I guess I should knock on wood for saying that."

A small laugh escaped her. "What's that saying? Life is what happens when you're making other plans?"

"I'd guess you know all about that."

She didn't answer. "Want any help?"

Boyd shook his head. "You relax and let me be useful. God knows I need it."

The sound of the TV still issued from the living room. Was that all that Herman had to occupy him? Sad.

Artie sat at the dinette watching him. "What did you mean when I asked where you were going?"

"Huh?" He glanced at her as he used a fork to scoop strips of bacon onto a paper towel.

"You said you were going the next mile."

Hell, he thought. How to explain that while revealing very little of his private demons? "Where do you want me to drain the excess bacon grease?"

"See that small white container near the stove? I keep it there for later use."

He snapped the lid off and tipped the frying pan, watching the grease pour into the container. "Good idea."

"And you're not answering my question."

A cop. He should have known she wouldn't let him slide past it. "I decided to walk from North Carolina to Washington state."

The toaster dinged. He set the pan on a cold burner, waiting for the temperature to reduce for the eggs, and turned to start another round of toast and to butter the current four slices.

"Why?" Artie asked. Inevitably, he thought.

"Because it seemed like the best way to deal with myself, okay?"

Boyd hadn't meant the words to sound harsh, but that's how they emerged. At least she didn't come back at him, questioning him more closely. Although to be honest about it, she had every right to know more about a stranger she'd brought into her home.

He diverted, returning to the current situation. A much safer topic than himself. "Any chance that motel might have a room today?" he asked.

She nodded toward the window. "What do you think? I'll call, but don't expect any escape, not today."

He began to scramble the eggs in the frying pan, topped by a layer of shredded cheese that melted into them. "It's not that I'm not grateful for your hospitality, because I am."

"But it's uncomfortable for all of us," she replied. "I get it. We'll just have to jolt along as best we can."

He stirred the eggs some more, keeping them from browning as they set up. "What happened yesterday?" he asked, even though it was none of his business. "Must have been bad."

She didn't answer until he started to scoop eggs onto the plates. "The worst case of domestic violence I've ever seen."

There was more, he was sure. "Want to get Herman? Or does he eat out there?"

"I'll ask him." She rose.

He pulled the last pieces of toast from the oven and slathered them with butter. Only then did it occur to him that not everyone here might like buttered toast. Oh, well.

Artie returned with Herman, who took his place. She brought out a jar of raspberry jam from the fridge and put it on the table, along with paper napkins. Soon the three of them made a triangle at the dinette.

Herman wasted no time diving in.

Artie politely commented on how good the eggs tasted. The bacon was perfectly done.

Idle chat because neither of them would move past it.

Sewed up tight in their own private hells, he thought. Well, they'd deal with silence today. Maybe one more day. They'd all survive it.

ARTIE WANTED TO do the dishes, but Boyd insisted he'd clean up. Taking the opportunity, she went to her bedroom and, sitting on her bed, opened her laptop again. At least the storm didn't appear to be interfering with the internet.

An answer had come from the office: Boyd had no record, no priors, no nothing. Prints showed he'd been in the Army until recently. The department had sniffed out that until two months ago he'd been employed at a construction company.

Not even a traffic ticket? The man was clean, maybe too clean, but records traced him all the way back to a birth certificate thirty-eight years ago.

Well, maybe he *was* clean as a whistle. Still, she didn't like his opacity. The guy was walking like this for a reason. His years at war? That was entirely possible.

Deciding she could look no further, she logged out of the department's connection.

Then she leaned back on her elbows and stared into empty space. She didn't want to be alone, she realized. She didn't want to let her thoughts keep spiraling around with only one destination. She wanted to be working, to be busy.

Except that she knew Gage was right, that she needed time to find the person she had buried late yesterday, to learn to live with the person she had discovered herself to be.

Her own actions kept her from taking any pride in saving the Lauer woman's life. Necessary actions to be sure, but they disturbed her deeply.

The only bruises weren't the ones on her body, that was for sure.

The wind still keened like a banshee. She didn't need to pull back the heavy curtains on her bedroom window to know the storm was still enjoying itself at a huge cost out there. She didn't need to look to know that it was unlikely she'd have even been able to patrol today. No, she would have been called out only if something bad happened, and she couldn't face another bad thing yet.

So what was she supposed to do? Anyone who thought stewing around inside your own head, while waiting for a psychologist to supposedly clean up the mess, was nuts.

But maybe diversion wasn't a good thing, either. Sooner or later she would have to face it.

Quietly growling, she sat up and tried to figure out what to do with this day. A stranger in her living room might have been a distraction, but he seemed as disinclined to talk as she was.

Not cool. He needed to tell her more about himself. Something other than that he'd taken it into his head to walk across the country. Talk about strange. People only did that when they were fundraising. To get headlines and TV coverage.

Boyd Connor did not strike her as someone who wanted any kind of attention. He was marching off something mile after mile. That backpack of his was carrying more than supplies.

She thought of her dad again, thought about how his life must seem to him now. He knew he was losing his memory, an awful thing to know. But on days like this, he couldn't seek activity at the senior center in the basement of Good Shepherd Church. He couldn't meet up with friends to pass the time with card games and conversation and endless coffee. He was stuck in this house with only the TV.

For a man who had been active all of his life, a man who had never been fond of watching TV except in brief spurts, this must feel like hell.

"Damn!" The word escaped her explosively and she jumped up.

Three people trapped by a storm that didn't show any sign of blowing itself out. One was a stranger.

Heck, she thought with an unexpected burst of amusement, didn't that sound like a plot for a movie?

Just as long as none of them stepped out into that blizzard to meet an axe killer.

Finally a laugh escaped her.

She was going to be okay.

ALTHOUGH BY EARLY AFTERNOON, she began to wonder if they *all* would be okay. Her dad started pacing the house restlessly. He was a man who needed physical activity, and sitting in front of the TV wasn't cutting it.

Artie watched him pace and wondered how many times he had paced for hours while she was at work, hours during which he might not have gone to the senior center for some reason. Maybe he sometimes forgot about going.

Realizing that neither she nor her father could be certain of his memory was a downer. More than once she'd thought about cutting off the gas to the stove because he might turn it on to make oatmeal or something else, then forget he had turned it on.

She *thought* he was used to using the induction coil, the air fryer, the coffeepot. But what if they slipped his memory, too?

Maybe she should scrape together the money to get an induction stove. At least it was less likely to cause a serious problem.

Damn it all. Worry forever nibbled at the edges of her mind but she wasn't ready to put her dad in a facility far away. It wasn't as if there was one near Conard City. Making time to visit him would be tough by itself.

And tearing him out of his home, the only house he'd ever lived in, might nearly kill him. It sure wouldn't make him happy.

He might even feel abandoned. Nor was his state bad enough to justify such a thing. No, she'd just have to keep on worrying about him and hoping he didn't deteriorate too fast or too much.

Home care? Maybe. If he could tolerate having someone to watch him all the time Artie was working.

Clara was a lifesaver, though. The two of them got on like a house on fire. The time they spent together plainly cheered Herman up. Clara seemed to enjoy it, too.

So she watched her father pace. Then Boyd took over part of the floor and began to do push-ups and squats. He clearly wasn't used to all this sitting, either.

Artie felt no urge to join them in the activity. Everything inside her felt drained, as if someone had pulled the plug.

Her dad, however, chuckled as he stepped around Boyd, who was busy working up a good sweat. He even teased the stranger in their midst. Artie couldn't help smiling when her father accused Boyd of being a masochist.

"That's one good word for it," Boyd retorted. "The other thing is I'm no layabout. Gotta keep moving."

Always moving, Artie thought, wondering about him again.

When the two men settled, Artie brought out a folding table and a pack of cards. Mental stimulation for her father. Distraction for her and Boyd.

Briefly the blizzard eased, but before hope of its end grew too much, it resumed blowing. Artie cussed as she heard the keening renew.

"Have you checked the motel for me?" Boyd asked quietly.

"Not yet. It'd be pointless anyway. As soon as the plows move through, the snow fills the roads again. We'd just get stuck out there trying to cross town. Only a fool would leave the La-Z-Rest while this is going on. How far would they make it out of town? Half a mile?"

She dealt another hand of cards and realized she hadn't been paying close enough attention to remember what game they were playing. In a moment of wryness, she wondered if her memory was going, too.

Then her cell rang. Hoping for word that she could hike her way into the office and answer phones or something, that one of the deputies with a plow on the front of his Suburban might show up to take her to work, she knew before she answered that no such word was about to arrive. The departmental vehicles with plows would be out in more distant areas to handle emergencies.

The voice she heard was unfamiliar.

"You're gonna get yours, Deputy. Better watch your back."

Then the caller disconnected. She checked her recent calls, but this one was labeled Unknown.

"What?" Boyd asked.

She hesitated, then answered truthfully, "I think

it was a threat." Then she shrugged. "I've had them before. No biggie."

Except she'd never had one over the phone. All the other threats had come in the middle of an episode, like a bar fight out at one of the roadhouses. A chill crept through her scalp and neck. Watch her back?

As if anyone could threaten her in this blizzard, she reminded herself. She pushed the threat aside and returned to the card game. Some bully. Bullies talked tough but seldom acted because they were cowards at heart.

Nothing to worry about. Hell, she didn't need one more damn thing to worry about.

FROM WHAT HE'D seen briefly in Artie's expression, Boyd knew she was more disturbed by the call than she was admitting. He wanted to know exactly what was said but couldn't ask.

In some ways this current situation was more than uncomfortable: it was annoying.

Herman, studying his cards, said, "Artie's name is special."

"Oh, Dad." Artie sighed.

"No, it's special. Your mom chose it specially." He lifted his gaze and looked at Boyd. "Letitia, my wife, had a thing for Greek mythology. I swear she could rattle off the entire pantheon without taking a breath. Could tell you what all the gods and goddesses represented."

"She could," Artie agreed. "She did it from time to time."

Herman smiled, his gaze growing distant with memory. "A smart woman, well read. She was always on me because I didn't read much."

"Because you were too busy as a mechanic," Artie said. "She always made you use that special soap."

"Three times at least. She wanted clean towels." Herman chuckled. "Had to use shop rags until she thought I was clean enough to use the good towels."

"And you complained every time."

Herman looked at her. "A working man gets dirty hands. Goes with the job."

"True." Artie folded her cards, clearly quitting the game.

Boyd spoke. "Letitia sounds like a wonderful woman."

Herman nodded. "She was. Always gentle. I can't figure out where Artie got her bristles and steel from."

"From you, Dad," she answered dryly. "Where else? But don't forget Mom had a strong backbone. She stood up to you, didn't she?"

Herman grinned. "That, too." Then he shook his head and proved he didn't forget everything that happened just minutes ago. "But Artie's name. Care to hear, Boyd?"

"Absolutely," Boyd said with a glance at Artie. "Unless she objects."

"Gonna tell you anyway. Letitia picked the name *Artemis*. Artie here has been spending most of her life trying not to use it. I think she hates that it's on her driver's license."

Artie sighed. "I don't hate it. It's just strange."

Boyd started to smile. "I like it. So, Herman, who was Artemis?"

"I'll never forget *that*," Herman answered. "Among other things, she was the huntress, the protector of nature. Figure how that goes together."

Artie clearly gave up. "Mom said that different towns and villages added traits to the gods and goddesses they most liked."

"That's right. I remember now." Herman nodded. "Anyway, she thought it was perfect for you, and I think she was right."

"Why?" Artie asked. "Do you think I wouldn't be me if she'd chosen another name?"

Herman laughed out loud. To his amazement, Boyd felt a grin on his own face. These two could be a trip. Even Artie had started to smile.

"Okay, I'm me," she said. "And the Romans stole Artemis and turned her into Diana. Why didn't Mom choose that name? It would have been easier to live with."

"Because Artemis was also the protector of animals, children and childbirth. I think she hoped you'd become a protector. And you did, didn't you?"

Artie didn't answer. Her face darkened. What was going on? Boyd wondered. Something about yesterday, whatever was troubling her? Something to do with being a protector?

Herman spoke again. "There's one trait I don't think your mom wanted you to have, though."

"Which is?"

Herman eyed her, then dropped a bomb. "Artemis was the goddess of virginity."

For endless seconds, except for the storm outside, you could have heard a pin drop. Boyd wished he could remove himself somehow. Make a quick bathroom call? Where had that statement come from and why had Herman mentioned it in front of him?

Artie sure as hell wished he'd kept his mouth shut. It was written all over her.

When she spoke, she kept her voice level. "Well, Dad, you don't have to worry about *that*."

It grew so quiet again that a pin drop would have sounded like a thunderclap.

All of a sudden, Boyd wished he could laugh. *These two.* They were something else.

Chapter Four

Dinnertime approached eventually. Artie wondered why she'd let her dad get her goat, but he sometimes had a way of doing that. The worst part was that she'd let him. And in front of Boyd. Why hadn't she just let it go?

Well, she hadn't. Her answer had flopped out there in a moment of annoyance and there it sat. Boyd Connor must be wondering if she was nuts.

Maybe she was headed that way. Especially after yesterday. She could feel the hair trigger of her emotions and had probably pulled it with that stupid announcement.

She hated to admit it, but Gage was probably right in not letting her come back to work yet. If she could respond to her *father* that way, simply because he'd irritated her, she shouldn't be driving around the county with a loaded Glock.

Hell, she was apparently loaded herself. Like a cocked pistol.

Pawing around in the pantry, looking for something to make dinner for the three of them, she paused a moment.

Nothing quick, she decided. The longer it took her to cook, the longer she could avoid her big faux pas. The gaze of a near stranger who didn't need to know such things about her. Oh, what was she thinking anyway? Boyd didn't need to know it, but he'd be leaving as soon as he could. It was her *dad* who didn't need to know that. For once, she hoped his memory problems would come to her rescue.

Leaning her head against a shelf, she knew she had to get a grip. Then there was Boyd. She could feel his desire to get on the move again. Whatever was tugging him along his trek wasn't easing any now because he was trapped by nature.

What the hell had happened to him anyway? What was *his* story?

She was used to living in an area where she knew most people and had all her life. Some acquaintances were just that, acquaintances. Some were people she wished she'd never had to meet, but they were a decided minority.

Regardless, she had a story of some kind or another about nearly everyone. Their families. Their troubles, their concerns, even their fears. The point was, she knew about them.

Now here she was with a man she knew almost nothing about, a man whose story was opaque to her, and she was uncomfortable with that. The guy didn't have any kind of pigeonhole.

It wasn't as if strangers never came to Conard

County. They did, of course. Many stayed long enough that their stories became known. Others moved on so fast it didn't matter.

But never had she taken in a true stranger. Never brought one into her home. So naturally she was uneasy.

Sighing, she straightened and started scanning shelves again. She had plenty of food stocked in her upright freezer on the mudroom, stocked against bad weather, or times when running to the grocery became difficult. She also had plenty of dry goods in her pantry. Cooking wasn't her favorite thing, but she could do it when Clara didn't run over to rescue her and her dad.

Only now she *had* to cook because she was damned if she was going to serve up frozen meals again. Because she needed to escape into a task that would require more than reading a label and punching buttons, or shoving it all into the oven to do the work for her.

Egad. How was she ever going to deal with her enforced leave from duty? But maybe it wouldn't be as bad when this blizzard blew itself out. At least she'd be able to get around, do things, see people.

A trickle of amusement came out of nowhere. And she thought Boyd was antsy? Look at her. Worse, look at her total self-preoccupation.

Sheesh.

She resumed her search but wasn't exactly thrilled with what she found. Okay, so it wasn't frozen meals, but the parts she'd have to put together would come mainly from boxes, like boxes of dried potatoes au gratin.

Suzy Homemaker she wasn't. Clean freak, yes, but chef, no.

Six cans of Spam? Seriously? Why so many? But she pulled one down anyway. Meat without thawing, which at this point in the day had become a requirement. Maybe she should thaw something for tomorrow?

Oh, heck, she thought, and put the Spam back on the shelf. Instead she got two boxes of red beans and rice, feeling certain she must have andouille sausage in the freezer to round it out. At least browning and slicing the sausage would require some of her degraded cooking skills. And a little time.

Was she really spending all this time thinking about cooking?

"Aagh," she groaned aloud. Was she coming to this?

"Everything okay?" Boyd's voice came from behind her.

It bothered Artie that she hadn't heard him approach. It bothered her that she was still standing in the pantry with the boxes in her hands. In an enclosed space where she could easily become trapped. "Red beans and rice okay by you?" she asked instead of answering his question.

"That's great. What can I do to help?"

Put him to use, she decided. He probably needed something to do as much as she did. Maybe even more.

"There's a freezer in the mudroom. Could you check and find a package of andouille sausage?"

"You got it."

She carried the boxes back into the kitchen and pulled out her rice maker from a lower cabinet. Another convenience. Another thing to keep her from standing over a stove. Hah!

Boyd returned with the package of sausage. "Success," he said. "Now what?"

"I need to thaw that. Could you put it unopened in a bowl of cold water?" She nodded to the cupboard with the larger bowls. Her mother's mixing bowls, some stainless steel and others glass.

"The whole package?"

"Yeah. Thanks. It won't take long." And while that thawed she would have to wait to make the rice. Great. Back into the pantry, but this time she emerged more quickly, with a box of blueberry muffin mix. Although she always turned it into a quick bread because it was easier.

The sausage was thawing and Artie pulled out a loaf pan. How many times had she watched her mother spend a day making bread dough, then turning a wonderful loaf out of that pan?

She grabbed another mixing bowl and started.

The silence was getting heavy again, she thought, so she spoke about something safe. "Do you know why I have to stand here adding eggs and other stuff to make a batter?"

He leaned back against the counter and folded his arms. "There's a reason?"

"Oh, yeah. My grandmother told me about it. Back when box cake mixes first appeared, all you had to do was add water. But the mix wasn't selling. Anyway, they finally figured out that women didn't feel like they were really baking when all the ingredients were already mixed. Success came when the companies altered the mixes so that anyone using them has to add eggs and oil and so on."

He tilted his head. "That's fascinating."

Artie merely shook her head. "It says something about women's roles at the time. Me, I'd be glad not to have to add anything but water."

Boyd chuckled, a pleasant sound. "I'd eat more baked goods if they were that easy to make."

While she was pouring the batter into the pan, he startled her with a question. "That phone call disturbed you, didn't it? But you say you get threats all the time."

She didn't want to answer. It seemed ridiculous to make a big deal out of a single phone call when she was perfectly able to look after herself. She answered anyway. No biggie, and she was getting tired of silences.

"Only that the threats I've received in the past have been in face-to-face confrontations. People get angry or drunk and say all kinds of things." She shrugged. "Just a bully wanting to make a point."

Boyd didn't reply immediately. It seemed to her that he frowned faintly. After a half minute or so he said, "I can see why that might be disturbing. I'd be disturbed."

Given his background, Artie doubted it. He'd faced

bigger threats than a phone call. One call was meaningless.

Until the next one came. Right after dinner.

DINNER TURNED OUT OKAY. The browned sausage, sliced neatly into bite-sized pieces, added some wonderful flavor. She'd made extra because of Boyd and his healthy appetite. The meal went over well and she was glad to see her dad eat heartily. Sometimes he seemed to forget to eat at all unless someone put food right in front of him.

If not for Clara, Artie would have spent all her time at work worrying about him. Maybe she should check on Clara again. A glance out the window, however, warned her that trying to get Clara over here would be difficult and maybe dangerous. In that wind with these low temperatures, people could get frostbite or hypothermia fast, especially older people like Clara.

She sighed.

Her dad spoke, becoming aware of something besides his meal. "Artie? What's wrong?"

"Being stuck in a blizzard is all. You know I'm not good at staying inside."

Herman smiled. "Never were. I used to have to pull you out of that tree in the backyard to get you inside for bedtime." He turned to Boyd. "Quite the tomboy."

"Quite the woman," Artie retorted. "Just because I was a girl didn't mean I wanted to be inside cooking and sewing."

Herman laughed. Boyd smiled.

"Anyway," Artie continued, "don't let your sexism show."

That drew another laugh from Herman. "Feminism started with your mother."

"In this house anyway."

Herman's gaze drew distant with memory, but his smile remained, although it had grown a bit sad. "I miss her, Artie."

"We both do," she answered quietly. Sorrow once again slipped into her heart.

"Sometimes I think she's going to walk back in the front door."

Artie stilled, wondering if he meant that literally or as a recognition of his grief. The former would be another step in the wrong direction. Man, this wondering was awful.

Then the landline rang. She looked up. Boyd looked at the phone. "Still have one of those landlines?" he asked.

"Cell towers out here aren't always reliable. The weather gets to them. But it has to be the sheriff. No one else has that number."

She rose, expecting to hear Gage Dalton's rough voice at the other end. Instead she heard a stranger.

"This is a warning," a male voice said. "We'll get you." Then he disconnected.

Okay. Now she couldn't dismiss the trickle of uneasiness that ran town her spine. Someone had gone to the trouble to get this phone number. Maybe someone serious. She closed her eyes briefly, trying to shake it off, then hurried to clear the table. *Keep busy.*

She might be stuck inside, but that didn't mean no one could get to her if they were determined enough. Her dad. She was more worried about him than herself, though. If someone tried to get into this house...

She couldn't complete the thought. She couldn't bear to. Images of herself running around to bar doors and check windows began to plague her.

She was not the type to worry excessively about her personal safety or she couldn't be in law enforcement. This was not the time to start, not because of two phone calls.

Boyd grabbed some of the remaining dishes and followed her to the sink with them. From the living room came the sound of the weather on TV.

"Another threat?" he asked quietly.

"Yeah. Meaningless."

She went back to get the last of the dishes, but Boyd forestalled her.

"I'll do the cleaning up, Artie. Least I can do. Go sit with your father."

And watch the unending, pointless broadcast.

It seemed to be enough for her father, though. He stared at the screen as if it were the most important thing in the world.

She wondered if he was trying to escape from his own condition or if he was really fascinated by that endless loop.

"How about a movie?" she asked him presently. "Something you want to see?"

"I want the Christmas tree."

"Okay," she answered promptly, although it was

the last thing in the world that she wanted to do. "I'll get it out of the attic."

"And those acrylic ornaments Letitia likes so much?"

His use of the present tense was another thing to trouble her. "Of course," she answered. "They meant so much."

Herman nodded. "She'll like that."

Boyd spoke from the kitchen doorway. "Need some help with the attic?"

"If you wouldn't mind." Ordinarily she would have asked one of her friends to help get that big, long box down. Too awkward for one person. It was about the only help she ever needed, though.

Her phone rang again, this time her cell. She didn't want to answer it after the earlier calls, but it could be the office. Maybe they needed some help despite her being on leave.

But it was Guy Redwing, one of her colleagues. "How are you and your dad getting by right now?"

"We're doing well." She watched Boyd put another log on the fire. He seemed to have taken over that chore. "You guys need any help?"

Guy chuckled. "Just can't stay away, huh? But there's little enough we can do right now. I hate to tell you how many deputies are stuck around the county right now. We'd better not have an emergency."

"Fingers crossed."

Guy's voice, usually unrevealing, grew warm. "You call if you need anything. We're bedded down around the office now. I got five people I can send over if you need anyone."

"Where's Gage?"

"The place any sensible man would be. At home."

Despite herself, Artie laughed. "What about the rest of you?"

"We're all nuts. You call, hear?"

"I will," Artie promised. She thought about mentioning the phone calls, then decided against it. It wasn't good for Guy to be sending someone over, not in this messy weather. Besides, she could take care of herself.

And if Boyd was half the man she'd begun to believe he was, he'd help protect Herman. She looked at him again and wondered if *stalwart* was a good description. It was beginning to seem like it.

He stood there waiting for the trip up to the attic. Putting down her phone, she led him to the back of the hallway. "Up there," she told him, pointing to the ceiling. "Drop-down ladder."

She usually had to get on a step stool to reach it. Boyd had no such problem.

He followed her up the ladder. She pulled the string that turned on three overhead lights and revealed the detritus of three generations. Old furniture, boxes full of items she couldn't remember because she'd never looked and they weren't labeled. Someday, she promised herself. An old promise she still hadn't kept.

"What needs to go down?" he asked.

She started pointing, and one by one she lowered boxes for him to reach for at the bottom and move out of the way.

"The tree is a beast," she warned him. "Mom

wanted this big one that's flocked with snow. Unfortunately, stringing the lights is practically a whole day's work."

Boyd came up to help her wiggle the box to the attic door.

"I'll catch at the bottom, okay?"

"No argument from me," Artie answered. "Just be ready for the weight."

The easy part was tipping the box over the edge and urging it to slide downward. Not nearly as easy on Boyd's end because he'd not only have to stop it at the bottom, but he'd have to slide it out of her way.

Naturally he made it look easy.

It only took a half hour to set the tree up in the corner where it had always stood, in front of seldom-used bookshelves. These days she read on her tablet.

"You know," she remarked, making casual conversation as they spread the branches, "I never read those books anymore. I have duplicates of the ones I love on my tablet."

"I would, too."

Would, not did. She wondered if he read at all. "Do you read much?"

"I used to. Lately I haven't felt much like it."

Again she pondered about his story. Again she wanted to ask. Again she didn't.

She began to pull lights out of the boxes. "These darn things get tangled even with the reels. I can't imagine how it happens."

One by one, they spread out strands and checked the miniature lights. All of them burned brightly. All of them blue. Just as her mom wanted. It was all just as her mom wanted.

And now just as her dad wanted, but this year he didn't help. This year he watched the weather.

Boyd was a great help, though. She never asked for help with this part. Because she ought to be able to decorate one damn tree by herself.

As soon as Boyd saw how she was trying to string the lights along each branch, just not once across each, he followed, helping with each strand. One tree and eight strands. It was always beautiful, though. The snow on the branches was clumped so that it didn't look artificial.

It was well worth doing, she admitted to herself. Every bit of it.

Putting it all away after New Year was when she wanted to rebel. Every year.

Amused, she realized she was smiling.

"This is fun," Boyd remarked.

"So you can still have fun?" The question maybe had more bite than she'd wanted.

He answered with apparent truth. "Occasionally. In patches."

Her, too, since her father's illness had become unavoidable, but she didn't say so. Instead, she said only, "This year I might be a Grinch."

"And that might be understandable."

Amazingly, with Boyd's help, the lights were on the tree by her dad's bedtime. He nodded approval as he passed by it. "Mom will like it. Great surprise for her."

Artie bit her lip, then said, "I'm sure she will, Dad."

After her father disappeared into his bedroom with the requisite checks from his daughter, Artie turned to Boyd, who was sitting on the floor. "I'm going to decorate this tree tonight, unless I'll keep you awake too late."

"Go for it," he answered. "It'll be a nice surprise for Herman in the morning."

BOYD, HOWEVER, had seen quite a bit that evening, and he was sorry as hell.

He hadn't missed the way Artie's father had shifted into the present tense when speaking of his late wife. Hadn't missed Artie's pained reaction, though she had tried to conceal it.

Then there were the threatening phone calls. Artie might pretend to shrug them off, maybe tried to tell herself they were meaningless.

But Boyd could read faces. He had spent a lot of time with people in tight-knit units. He'd learned to tell when some guy's game face tried to conceal that he was about to crack. To tell when someone was growing more fearful than usual. To know when someone seriously needed a break. At his rank, he'd been something of a father to all of them.

A better father to his unit than to his daughter. He yanked himself away from that black hole and focused on his present circumstances. He was also good at that when necessary.

Right now he was seriously worried about Artie.

The thing with her father couldn't be helped. That was happening regardless.

But those threatening calls? He wasn't about to dismiss them. For the first time he considered how to remain in this house if Artie didn't get protection from her fellow officers. If she never told them about the calls so she wouldn't *get* that protection. He wouldn't put it past her. To him she seemed too self-reliant. Too unwilling to seek help even for something that might be a serious threat, or she would have called already. She'd have told that officer who called earlier.

He felt sorrow for her, for having to watch her father fail like this.

Watching Artie open the boxes of tree ornaments, he decided he might have to be her protector. Lousy at protection as he was, given the situation with his daughter.

Self-loathing rose in him again, bringing bile to his throat. Well, he might be able to do a better job here, at least for a brief time.

Then he rose from the floor. "What can I do to help?"

Boyd woke to an excited exclamation in the morning before the sun came up. He sat up immediately and looked around. He found Herman standing in front of the tree, wearing a tattered old plaid robe, smiling from ear to ear.

Artie appeared quickly, still tying her black robe around her waist. "Dad?"

"The tree," he answered. "Pretty like it always is. I guess Letitia finished it while I was sleeping."

Oh, God, Boyd thought. Artie appeared to nearly shrivel. He felt renewed pain for her. The blizzard still raged outside, but he felt as if it had come indoors. A storm. For an instant it all brewed inside.

ARTIE FELT EVERYTHING inside her clench at the way her father was speaking about her mother. God! Was it getting worse? Was he slipping his place in time more often? How could she be sure?

These instances had been happening for a while, but were they coming closer together? Or had the approach of Christmas, heralded all over the TV, simply triggered the problem?

Taking Herman to the doctor and to a therapist wasn't very helpful. Crosswords? Herman had always hated them. No word games for him. Memory puzzles? If she could keep him working on them for longer than two minutes.

She went to stand beside her dad, staring at the tree. "It's beautiful, isn't it?" She couldn't bring herself to join him in his belief that her mother would return at any moment. Trying to jostle him back into the present would only make him furious.

Maybe it was better to just let him enjoy his happiness right now. God, how did she know? She just didn't want to anger him or hurt him. Either would be awful.

After a few minutes, she looked at Herman and said, "I'm going to make breakfast. You hungry?"

He nodded, still staring at the tree. "Oatmeal."

"You got it." There were plenty of packets of the

instant stuff in her pantry because her dad liked it so much. Personally, she hated it.

Boyd followed her, still dressed in the gray sweatshirt and pants he must have slept in. Socks on his feet.

"What can I do?"

For an instant she felt angry. He was so underfoot with his offers to help. So at loose ends, reminding her that she was at loose ends, too.

"Slice the blueberry bread for me?"

"Gladly. Will your dad eat any?"

"If it's there," she answered quietly. "If it's there. Do you like oatmeal?"

"Love it."

"Then you and Dad make a club of two. I hate it. I don't like any hot cereals."

More pointless conversation. This was going to drive her mad, although in the current situation she didn't know how she could escape it.

As she served oatmeal for the two men and blueberry bread for herself, she remarked, "I wonder if this storm is ever going to blow through."

Now reduced to talking about the weather. She closed her eyes briefly, then went to get her father.

It occurred to her that she wasn't being a very nice person. Not since the domestic. Not since Billy Lauer. Not since she was facing a truth: she hadn't swung her baton simply to protect Bea Lauer. She'd raised it in rage.

She'd lost her self-control.

TWO MEN, Willie and Joe Lathrop, hunkered down in their small house far outside town.

"Time to make another call?" Willie asked he stirred the embers of the fire on the hearth.

Joe shook his head. "Tain't smart, Willie. I could git in more trouble."

"How? That cop's gonna testify against you, and you'll get years for a bar fight? Mack's angry, too. She took away his license. Now Billy Lauer. You gonna let her testify against him, too?"

Billy was a good friend of theirs. They didn't exactly approve of the way he beat Bea, but they could see the sense in it. Damn woman wouldn't stay in line for nothin'.

Joe said, "Cop bashed Billy up pretty good, too, from what I'm hearin'."

The men poured some more coffee from the tin pot resting on the stones in front of the fire. They had some standards. No beer before noon. Maybe.

"We gotta stop her from testifying," Willie said firmly. "Scare her off."

"She don't seem like the type to scare easy."

"We'll do it. Just gotta keep on."

"Call some of the others that's mad," Joe said finally. "See what they think about it."

Willie scratched his head and rocked in the old wood chair. "We know what they think. Mack's still seeing red. Ain't nothin' changed."

Joe shook his head. "I mean about another call this soon."

Willie grunted. "Mack said to make some calls, maybe scare her."

"I mean it, Willie. We might could do this all wrong."

"We got good enough heads."

"Remember what Ma used to say? About more heads being better?"

Willie grunted again. "Okay, okay." But he sounded more annoyed than agreeable. "You remember we might have to do more."

"I 'member. Can't hardly forget."

The beer came out early, as soon as they finished their coffee.

Chapter Five

In the late afternoon, the wind quieted down like a baby who was through screaming. Outside, some snow still fell, but not much. Behind them, a movie ran on the big-screen TV. Something with sled dogs abandoned in an Antarctic winter. Herman had asked for it.

"Looks like the storm is almost over," Boyd remarked as he stood beside Artie at the front window.

"The weather said three days. But you must be in a rush to get out of here. Not that I blame you."

Surprisingly enough, he wasn't. Why, he couldn't really say. Something about that protector urge, which might not even be necessary since another call to Artie had failed to come. Or was it something else? He sure didn't seem to be able to avoid noticing how attractive Artie was. She'd probably hate him if she knew.

Then the wind screamed again and almost instantly the house across the street disappeared in the whirlwind.

"I thought it was about to stop," he remarked.

"I don't know, but this looks like a whiteout. You know, when the snow is dry enough that it blows around. It's hell when it hits and you're on the road."

Since he could no longer see the house across the street, he knew she was right. And he'd seen whiteouts in Afghanistan.

She turned her head and offered him a crooked smile. "As long as these keep happening, no one should move anywhere. Although if the blowing stops long enough, people might think it's safe to go out in their cars. It might not be."

She turned to look back out the window. "It just takes a few strong gusts and there it is."

As well he knew from experience, but he didn't tell her so. She was talking, not silent with worry, and he didn't want to stop her. "But no one can stay hunkered down all winter."

"No. When the sun comes out again it'll help, hardening the snow on top. Until then…" She shrugged. "Guess you're stuck here a little longer."

Which was far from the worst fate, Boyd thought. Awkward as it was for him, and for Artie, he had no desire to hit the road again. Not yet.

Besides, he could get the phone calls he was hoping for as well from here as from the road. He just couldn't hike out his roiled emotions, not when he was here.

Artie's cell phone rang. She answered it without hesitation, maybe because she could read the name of the caller. She put it on speaker. "Hi, Clara. How are you making out?"

"I'm doing just fine. I wanted to ask about that old man of yours."

"Oh, he's doing great. Watching one of his favorite movies, happy the Christmas tree is up."

"Is that Clara?" Herman asked. "I know that voice."

Artie closed her eyes. "Yes, Dad, it's Clara. Want to talk to her?" But Herman just went back to his movie.

After a pause, Clara said, "Like that, huh?"

"Sometimes. We're okay, though. And you stay tucked inside."

"Saw the whiteout. I am *not* going to attempt to shovel my walk."

Artie laughed. "I'd recommend that."

"You shovel that dang stuff and it just blows into a heap nearby anyway, and the heaps keep getting deeper."

"I've noticed that."

"I think we all have," Clara said dryly.

"When are you going to hire someone with a snow-blower?"

"It's getting sooner with every year. This may be the year. I'm getting tired of it. Thinking about Florida. Not seriously, though."

"I'm glad to hear that."

When Artie disconnected, she almost seemed to relax. One concern off her mind, Boyd supposed.

Then he spoke. "I'll walk to the grocery when this lightens. You need some fresh veggies. Other things. Give me a list."

She tilted her head and wasn't smiling. "What did I say about not going out until the sun crusts the snow?"

He looked out the window again. "If it'll make you feel better, I'll wait until tomorrow. But I've been through this before." He turned his attention to her again.

"And just how much will you be able to carry in that backpack of yours?"

"I'll manage. Get me a list from Clara, too."

A snowplow groaned its way past on the street, as they had been nearly since the start of the blizzard. Waging a tireless and mostly useless battle to keep streets clean enough for emergency vehicles.

Boyd spoke. "I imagine they're plowing outside town, too."

"They are. But do you have any idea how many hundreds of miles of road there are out there? They keep the plows stationed at intervals along the state highway to make it faster, but it's still going to be a while."

She faced him. "Talking about going to the grocery? You're not planning to leave in the morning, then?"

"No." But he didn't tell her why, because she'd be furious if she knew he was staying out of concern for her. "I'll get a room at the motel as soon as one becomes available." Even though that would put him too far away from the current situation, but if it helped Artie to be more comfortable, he'd find another way to keep an eye on her.

Her lips compressed. "Like hell," she said. "Like hell."

He didn't pursue the matter. No point. But he was relieved she didn't seem to be in a hurry to throw him out.

ARTIE LOOKED AT the stranger in her home, still wondering about his story. So he knew whiteouts? She hadn't felt as if she was giving him any new information, so why had she rattled on?

The movie was over. Her dad began pacing again. She couldn't bear to watch it. He always looked so alone when he did it. Memories? His despair over his diminishing capabilities? She didn't know how to ask, or if she should. Always that tightrope between dealing and hurting.

At least he paused occasionally to look at the tree. His face relaxed when he did. Was he still expecting Letitia to come through the door? If so, he didn't appear distressed by the fact that she hadn't yet.

She went to the kitchen to make some more coffee and try to plan another meal. God, she wasn't good at meal planning, either. She'd been able to justify it because of work, but there was no justification now.

Boyd came with her. "Thinking about dinner?"

"How did you guess?" Her voice held an edge of bitterness. She hated the sound of it.

"Why don't you let me root around? Maybe I can cook it tonight."

"When did you become a chef?"

One corner of his mouth tipped up. "No chef. It was just survival."

"Have at it." Her voice sounded more natural this time.

A few minutes later, he emerged from her pantry with a jar of chipped beef. "This and cream gravy? On toast?"

She noted he didn't use the military slang for it. Probably because he didn't want to use the impolite word in front of her. As if she hadn't heard it a million times. "Sounds good. My dad loves it. He doesn't get it often because I'm lousy at making cream gravy."

He nodded. "Takes a little practice. Anyway, you're getting low on bread. You wouldn't happen to have one of those machines?"

Her personal nod to her mother's homemade bread. She almost never used it and felt like a slug for not kneading the dough herself. "I have one." Down in the cabinet with the rice cooker.

"How long does it usually take?" he asked, looking at the clock. "Because I'll be using your last loaf."

"An hour and a half maybe. Or two. I can't remember."

"Good enough. It'll be ready soon enough for morning."

"Have at it." She pulled out the machine and told him the recipe was inside it. Then she started moving toward the living room to check on her dad. To avoid seeing a stranger in the most comforting room in the house.

Boyd's voice stopped her. "Artie? What happened that got you put on a leave?"

Internally, she swore. Quite inventively. "How is it any business of yours?"

"It's not. But I can tell you were upset when you picked me up. Saved me from myself, maybe."

Well, she didn't want to talk about it. She shifted direction. "You can't possibly carry many clothes in that backpack of yours, big as it is. I can show you my washer and dryer."

"I'm used to grungy clothes." Then he chuckled. "Of course, you might not like the smell. Thanks."

Then Artie at last made her escape to the living room. To one of the most troubling problems in her life.

Used to grungy clothes? She added that tidbit to the story she was beginning to build about him.

Then she returned to her dad. The movie was long over and he was watching cartoons again. She ought to be grateful he still remembered how to use the remote. Maybe the memory was so old that it didn't leave him.

The complexity of Alzheimer's was difficult to grasp. The death sentence it gave him troubled her beyond bearing.

"Dad? Would you like another movie?" Even in his state he must be growing sick of cartoons. But maybe the simplicity of them gave him some pleasure without taxing him.

"A Christmas movie," he said presently. "One your mother likes."

So the slippage in time continued. Maybe Christmas wasn't such a good idea after all.

Boyd had the chipped beef soaking and was putting ingredients in the bread machine when the wall phone rang. He looked up as Artie came to stand before it. At least he hadn't put the flour in with the liquids yet.

She stood for a few seconds looking at the phone, then answered it.

"Jackson," she said briefly.

Not long after, he saw her face pale. Okay, this was going beyond enough.

She hung up with a slam.

"What was that?" he asked.

Instead of telling him it was none of his business, she answered sharply, "Another damn threat. This time the creep said it could get worse than phone calls."

Boyd forgot the bread. This was indeed beyond enough. "Damn it, Artie, you can't keep ignoring this."

"Just a creep. A coward hiding behind phone calls. They're easy enough to make." But her color hadn't returned.

"You keep telling yourself that. But it isn't quitting. Could it have anything to do with that incident before you picked me up?"

"*That* beast is still in jail."

"How do you know?"

"Because of the blizzard. Nobody's going to make it to court in this mess. Not his lawyer, not the prosecutor, not the judge. They probably won't arraign him until tomorrow or the next day."

"That's a bail hearing?"

"Yeah, and possibly a plea. Which will be *not guilty* because he's such a bastard he probably doesn't think he's done anything wrong."

"I've known that type. Total sociopaths."

Now he saw the unspoken questions on her face. She didn't need to know about *him*. There was a more pressing matter anyway. "You need to call your department. Tell them about this."

"Like hell. I can take care of myself."

"Like hell," he retorted. "Not when you don't know what's going on."

Anger seeped out in her voice. "What can they do about some damn phone calls? God, Boyd, you're making a mountain out of a molehill."

He'd had enough. "I've also been in situations where I had to depend on the eyes and ears of other people! They might have some ideas. They have more resources than you do at home."

"They're already overstretched and this storm is creating a mess for them," she snapped at him. "Stay out of my business!"

Then she stormed out of the kitchen.

That was it, Boyd decided. Nothing was going to drag him away now.

He wondered if she'd even considered that her father might be at risk, too. That he might be the one most at risk. There were a lot of ways to get to someone.

HERMAN WAS INVOLVED in *Miracle on 34th Street*, the original version. A movie Artie had once loved, too. Now it held reminders of grief, reminders of how much her mother enjoyed it. Mom had always put it on at a time when there would be no interruption and, if there was one, life would have to wait.

Grief stalked her footsteps, Artie sometimes thought. Grief about the past, grief about the now, grief about the future.

She shook herself and watched a bit about Santa playing Santa at the department store. About the little girl who spoke Dutch, which Santa of course understood.

Then she thought ahead to the courtroom scene. A moment when sheer joy would burst from the video. She wished she could find something like that in a real court.

But then her thoughts darkened again, remembering Billy Lauer, about the merciless way he was treating his wife when she found them. About her own damn baton. Couldn't she have handled it better?

She closed her eyes, hating to remember it, but unable to stop second-guessing herself. Moment by moment she replayed the entire atrocity, wondering what she could have done differently.

There had to have been a better way. But Lauer had seemed hell-bent on killing his wife. Beating her bloody wasn't enough. Nothing would have stopped him from strangling Bea. She wondered if she could have pulled him off. But even one hit from her baton hadn't stopped him. It had taken repeated blows for him to turn his fury on Artie.

With her eyes closed, she could still see Bea with only a few seconds left in her miserable life. The blood. Lauer's hands squeezing the breath from her.

God, what made people do things like that? She could understand a drunken brawl. Tempers fueled by booze. Anger during a squabble between neighbors that resulted in blows, usually after the quarrel had been going on for a long time. Usually because nobody would compromise.

This was different. Something in Lauer wasn't right.

Was dangerously wrong. Something in him made him an innate murderer. Who might he take that rage out on when he could no longer get at Bea?

But he couldn't be the one threatening Artie. He was locked in a cell where he'd probably had his one phone call. His only phone call. A phone call that wasn't even required by law. A courtesy only.

Maybe the deputies who'd arrested him had been mad enough to refuse that call.

It was possible.

She opened her eyes, unable to find a resolution to her conundrum. She hated what she'd done, but she didn't have to hate herself for failing to find another way.

Behind her, Santa Claus was still insisting he was Santa Claus. What came next to entertain her dad? *How the Grinch Stole Christmas*? Why not. A better cartoon for her father than the silly ones he'd been watching.

When the aroma of baking bread reached her, she returned to the kitchen.

BOYD HEARD HER light footsteps as she approached. He glanced at the clock and saw it was almost time to begin toasting the remaining loaf of bread and making the cream gravy. But that wasn't critical.

His sense of urgency had grown. This woman needed some kind of help to deal with the mess on her plate, but he couldn't imagine what. Her dad's disease was inevitable. Whatever had happened to her on the job was bad enough she'd been placed on leave. All he could do was hang around waiting for some way, any way, to help.

Her face was smooth but her eyes were pinched. "That baking bread smells really good," she said.

"I love the smell. I ought to get one of these machines eventually."

"See what you think when you taste the results. When I get around to it, I only make simple white bread."

"Hot and fresh, it's the best."

More dancing around. Artie sat at the table, chin in hand, and simply stared. At him. At empty space.

LATER, AFTER A dinner that had pleased Herman enough to eat two huge helpings, Artie insisted on doing the dishes.

Boyd left her to it, saying only that he wanted to step outside for a few minutes, just to see how the weather was doing.

But what he needed to do was make a phone call to his ex-wife, Shelley, to find out how Linda was. Not that he expected any good news. He'd made Shelley promise to call when matters improved, but she hadn't called and the demons riding his back wouldn't let him trust for long.

The connection went through. He waited through six rings, his heart sinking with each one, his stomach knotting. Had something else happened?

But then Shelley answered, sounding impatient. "I told you I'd call, Boyd."

He closed his eyes, ignoring the frigid wind that

blew around the porch, its fury blinding with dry snow. No improvement there, either.

"Shelley, I just need an update, about everything."

"Like you wanted updates ever before."

Bile rose in Boyd's throat. That wasn't entirely true, but he let it pass. He didn't want an argument, but he still needed news.

"Look," Shelley said. "I'm not going to pressure her. She's under enough pressure. She's torn up enough. She still doesn't want to press charges."

Boyd's breath locked in his throat. Before long, he could find some air. It was so cold it made him want to cough. "I think I can understand that."

"I'd like her to realize that putting this damn man behind bars would make her feel better."

"A trial might not."

Shelley's voice tightened. "How dare you? You aren't here, you were never here! You don't have a right to an opinion!"

His hand tightened around his cell phone until his fingers might have crushed it. "The counseling?"

Shelley's anger shot across the miles. "She still doesn't want to see you. The psychologist says a lot of that may have to do with you being a man. Your long absences didn't help, either. Linda doesn't trust you."

He drew a shuddering breath. "Got it."

"Anyway, I know you, Boyd. It might make things worse for Linda if you get here feeling like you want to tear Seattle apart. Deal with your own mess. You're not ready to help with anyone else's."

Boyd closed his eyes. There was more than his

fury he needed to deal with, but he didn't mention it. They were his problems, not something he needed to burden anyone else with. And yeah, he still wanted to rip things apart. Drop bombs. Clear out every sleaze who occupied that city.

Then she floored him. "How's your PTSD?"

He answered frankly, "I don't have room for it now."

"I don't know if I should be glad about that. I remember how it could get."

So did he. "Don't worry about it."

"Well, you sure took a helluva way to deal with all this. I keep feeling you're bearing down on us like a rocket-propelled grenade."

He gritted his teeth so hard his jaw hurt. Then he squeezed out the words. "Tell Linda I love her."

Shelley disconnected without another word, the silence on the line as deafening as a bomb.

After the call, Boyd remained on the front porch, risking frostbite, letting the icy wind batter him. It was all he deserved.

But soon the door behind him opened and he heard Artie's voice.

"Boyd, get in here. I don't want to be dealing with any frozen corpses."

What an invitation, he thought as he turned. *That woman!*

She sparked a lot of things inside him, not all of them bad. In fact, little about her was bad at all.

Amazing.

Unlike his phone call with Shelley.

WILLIE AND JOE LATHROP remained hunkered down in the ramshackle house they'd inherited. From experience, neither of them needed to know that the wind was probably building a drift six or more feet high on one side of the house, and probably around the front corner, too. Onto the porch.

Both knew they'd be fools to leave the house. Even after it all settled, neither of them was going to want to try to tunnel out. Sometimes Joe remarked that they might as well stay put all winter.

Impossible, of course. Plenty of food in the house, though. Plenty of coffee and beer, too. Even a couple bottles of whiskey for times when longnecks weren't enough. But not for all winter.

Worst of it was their phone wasn't working. Not the landline or the cells. No more calls to that cop, not now.

Willie popped the top on another beer. Joe tossed a log onto the fire. No central heat in this old house.

They were pretty much stuck together in this one room unless one of them ventured to the kitchen for peanut butter and crackers. Tempers might fray, but from long practice they knew not to take it too far with each other.

"Can't even call Mack," Joe muttered.

"What good'll that do? We can't git outta here, we can't make a call. Mack's prolly stewing as much as we is and he still thinks we're fools."

"Can't argue that." Joe took another swig of his beer. "Woulda liked a football game or somethin'."

Both men stared at the big flat-screen that had

betrayed them early during the blizzard. The only splurge they'd made in this place.

"Lucky we still got power," Willie said.

"Can't figure that out nohow. No landline but we still got power?"

"I'm not complainin'."

"Nah. Just seems weird is all."

"Got that right."

More silence. More beer guzzled.

Then Joe spoke. "I keep sayin' we need a woodstove. Less wood to chop every year."

"Got any idea how much they cost?"

"I ain't no fool. Seems like I was with you when we looked. Don't mean we don't need one."

Willie nodded. He'd started thinking about their whiskey stash. "We can't do nothin' about that damn cop right now."

"They's time," Joe answered. "Court ain't for a coupla weeks now."

Willie nodded. "Time. But they ain't too much of it." He rose. "How about some *real* booze while we do some thinkin' about that cop."

BOYD AND ARTIE sat up after Herman went to bed. Before them on the TV, the weather station chatted cheerily about more hellish weather. This was one blizzard that wasn't going anywhere in a hurry, probably one to be talked about for years to come.

They sipped brandy. Artie enjoyed the blaze from the fire. Ordinarily she'd rely on the central heating, but Boyd seemed content to keep loading the fireplace, and it *was* more cheerful than anything else around here.

Well, the Christmas tree added some cheer, too. Especially now that Herman had moved back into the present.

Boyd eventually spoke quietly. "How bad is it with Herman? Or just tell me to mind my own business."

Artie shook her head. Boyd was seeing it. Hardly a secret. "I can't really be sure. No one can. A year ago he started having problems with recent memories. Conversations we had that he'd totally forget two days later. But it wasn't often."

"And now?"

"More often. And you've seen it, those slips into the past. They're a recent development. No one can tell me how fast this is going to worsen. Nobody. Varies with everyone, everyone has their own slope. For periods he's just fine."

"And you live for them."

Artie nodded. "I sure do." She looked straight at him, feeling the corners of her mouth tug down. "I'm already starting to miss him."

"That's gotta be hell."

"Pretty much. If I didn't have so many wonderful memories of when he was himself it might be easier." Her hand shook slightly and she put her brandy on the side table. "I've got to cling to *that* man. Hang on to those good days. I don't want to lose them. I've also got to cling to what I still have with him. Much harder." The true hell of it. Today versus yesterday. Both important.

Boyd nodded and fixed his gaze on the fire.

Well, Artie thought, what could he say? Nothing. Not for something that no one could help.

BOYD STARED INTO the fire, thinking over his phone call with Shelley. She'd reminded him of every one of his failures. She'd brought up his PTSD, not that she'd ever evinced a smidgen of sympathy for it. No, it had frightened her and angered her and he couldn't blame her for that.

But she'd brought it up. A spear meant to pierce him, then that bit that she felt like he was an RPG aimed at her.

God, was that really how he made her feel? Just by walking across the country, hoping like hell that Linda would reach the point where she wanted to see him? Hating himself with each stride for all his failures?

And if that was how Shelley felt, how could he ever be sure that she'd allow Linda to see him? To allow Linda to trust him enough to *want* to see him?

For the first time it occurred to him that he might be on a true fool's errand. In the end it might not be Linda's feelings about him, but Shelley's that would prevent him from hugging his daughter.

What in the hell could he possibly do about that? How could he know if, or when, it might be safe to find a way to approach Linda? He was being held behind a solid steel wall, and despite Shelley's earlier promises that she would let him know when Linda was ready to see him, he could no longer believe in them.

She had just stripped him of his last hope.

Working his jaw, he stared into the fire, facing a hopelessness that wasn't new to him. Just a new kind.

But he was damned if he was going to give in to it.

First he was going to settle in his own mind that these threats Artie was getting were just blather. That she was really safe from harm. That her dad was safe, too. He was growing fond of the old man as well as Artie.

Then he was going to resume his trek to Seattle and figure out what to do once he got there. Once he had dealt with the demons inside him.

As Linda's legal father, as a father with shared custody, there had to be ways around the wall Shelley was building.

If indeed she *was* building a wall. How the hell could he know? Nasty comments didn't necessarily mean a permanent state of affairs. Shelley was under a lot of strain after all.

But he still wanted to hurl his brandy glass against the hearth and listen to the satisfying sound of it shattering.

He closed his eyes and drew a deep breath.

That was *exactly* the person he never wanted to be again.

Focus on Artie and Herman. There must be something useful he could do here.

Chapter Six

Artie sensed the terrible tension in Boyd since that phone call he'd made from the front porch. He'd returned with a darkened face, a stiffness to his posture she hadn't seen before.

In fact, until then he'd turned into a comfortable companion, one who left her alone with her self-disgust, her struggle with capabilities she'd never suspected in herself. A painful journey to acceptance.

Gradually, despite all that, she'd felt a growing awareness of him as a man. An attractive man, despite him being bottled up as tightly as she was at the moment.

In the midst of all this she could feel sexual attraction? Once again she wanted to shake her head at herself. Talk about an emotional mess. Her brain felt as if it had been in a blender since the Lauer incident. Her gut, too, come to that.

But wanting sex with this stranger? God, she was losing it. Or maybe the idea of a stranger felt safer. He'd be moving on as soon as the storm and travel conditions would allow. No continuing complications.

She had enough complications in her life just then.

Sighing, she rose and went to refresh her brandy. She spoke to Boyd, who had grown even more silent than usual. "Would you prefer a beer or more brandy?"

He looked toward her. "Beer?"

She shrugged. "I keep it for when the guys drop by. Never liked it myself. But maybe you'd prefer it. I didn't think to ask."

"I'm hardly an invited guest," he answered dryly. "But a beer would be great."

She didn't keep the beer in the fridge but on a closed shelf against the wall of the mudroom. Just inside the kitchen so it wouldn't freeze but it wasn't taking up room in her small fridge. She brought him an icy bottle and returned to her seat. For some reason, despite the growing lateness of the hour, she felt no desire to turn in.

The heat from the fire felt welcome after her venture into the colder kitchen.

Boyd surprised her then by speaking once again of the off-limits topic. "Artie? What's had you so upset since you picked me up? Why did you get put on leave with pay?"

She nearly glared at him. "Suppose you tell me about that phone call that upset you so much?"

"Touché," he answered after a half minute. "I guess we both got our own secrets."

"Seems like." Feeling grumpy now, all relaxation gone, she scowled. "Why'd you have to bring that up?"

His voice took on an edge. "Because you've been getting threats."

She drew a deep breath, seeking her self-control, usually an easy thing, but suddenly difficult. Her own voice grew sharp. "Has it occurred to you that all those calls have come since you got here?"

Chapter Seven

Oh, hell, Boyd thought, feeling almost gut-punched. There it was. An idea that hadn't occurred to him but had sure occurred to her. How could he answer without telling her too much about himself? How could he reassure her? Her accusation filled the air like a suffocating smog.

Then the moment of shock clarified. "You know I haven't been making those calls. Have you seen me use my phone? Haven't I been here when you received every call? Do I somehow know the number of your landline? It's sure not written on the phone. What could I have against you anyway?"

She didn't answer, but she didn't look at him, either.

"I'm on a mission," he said presently. God, with this woman worrying about everything else she didn't need to be worrying about a threat inside her own walls. "I've got one thing on my mind and it isn't you. You know damn well I only just met you, and there's nothing on your official records about me being any kind of danger to you—or to anyone else. In fact, I'm the biggest threat to myself." It hurt to admit that, but it was true. Too true.

"You're the invisible man, like I said."

"Is that what has you worried?" He was certain it was, and he ached as he realized he wasn't going to be able to remain invisible with this woman. The urge to move on was growing again. His demons were his own.

"All I know is you spent too much time in Afghanistan. That you have medals and a reasonably high rank and that you're retired with disability. That you had a job with a construction firm you quit two months ago."

His fists began clenching. "That's quite a bit, don't you think?"

"You know a hell of a lot more about me."

"Do I? I know you're a cop, I know where you live and I know your dad now. That's not much."

"You think not? Where do you live? Where's your family? What do you do now except trek around like a nomad?"

This was probably not a good time to continue this conversation, Boyd thought. He was knotting up inside again. Getting up and walking away, even out into the storm, seemed like a good idea. Just go and never return.

Except some kind of tendril seemed to be growing between him and Artie. Some need on his part to ensure she was okay. A need to help in ways he couldn't help his own daughter.

A need to be something more than a useless guy

trying to walk off bottomless rage and a sense of failure that would haunt the rest of his life.

"Okay," he said finally. "Okay."

"Okay what?"

"I was in Afghanistan. You read that. Too many times, maybe. I was good. Maybe too good. There was a crying need for experienced NCOs."

Once again she put her brandy snifter on the table beside her chair, this time twisting to look at him. "That war has been endless."

"Until lately. You've heard they call it a generational war?"

She shook her head. "No. What's that mean?"

He wanted to throw his beer bottle. His hand clenched around it until it should have shattered. "It means," he said heavily, "that I found myself leading young men and women whose fathers and mothers I had served with. Did I know who they were? Hell, yeah." He drew a deep, steadying breath. "Kids. Following their parents into uniform and the same damn war."

"Oh, my God," she murmured.

"Yeah. *Oh, my God.* Almost nobody thinks about it that way. Almost nobody. I thought about it every damn day for the last few years of my career. It might not have been so awful if some of these troops hadn't been only four or five when the damn war started. Hell, a few of them had barely been toddlers back at the beginning."

"I can't imagine," she said quietly.

"I didn't have to imagine. I saw it too often. Frankly,

Artie, it haunts me." There. He admitted to it. To someone, for the very first time. He had a lot of ugly, brutal memories stamped into his mind, but that one… that one brought an infinite sorrow of a different kind.

"I'm so sorry, Boyd." Then she asked, "Is that why you're on this hike?"

"I've got a lot of things to deal with, but I didn't need to deal with that one by walking."

"So this is different?"

"Yeah." He had no intention of telling her more than that. She didn't need to know about his daughter, about his abject failure as a father. That Linda didn't even want to see him.

Nobody needed to know that outside Shelley, Linda and himself. Well, and her counselor, apparently.

Time to turn the tables on her. "Your turn," he said. "What the hell is going on apart from Herman?"

"You don't need to know."

"Maybe not. But you didn't need to know that about me, did you?"

She shook her head, looking down as if she never wanted to raise her head again. Serious trouble, he judged.

"Artie?" He kept his voice quiet. "Do you think you've seen or done anything I haven't?"

Her head jerked up at that. Despite the glow from the firelight, he saw her face pale.

"Something got you put on leave," he said. "I heard the call. Leave with pay. That usually means a terrible event. That you were involved in violence. Am I right?"

She rose from her recliner and began pacing. "I don't want to think about it."

He nodded, leaning back, making himself as unthreatening as he could. "I can sure understand that."

"So you talk about it?" she demanded, turning on him.

"I just did."

"How can you talk about it without thinking about it?"

"You can't." He waited, knowing she might not speak another word to him, but determined not to press her any further.

One thing for sure, he was hurting for her. With all his problems, he hadn't become immune to feeling for others. He had the worst urge to reach out, just draw her into his arms, encircle her in a hug. As if that would do her a damn bit of good. Embraces were hardly a bulwark against an internal enemy.

"Okay," she said finally, still pacing. "When I picked you up, I'd just come from the most horrific domestic violence scene I'd ever responded to." Her arms now wrapped around herself, holding herself tightly.

"Pretty remarkable you gave a damn about me," he offered. Maybe it would remind her that not everything was violent. Although he knew damn well that little could erase brutality.

"It's my job," she said sharply, facing him at last. "Like I was going to leave you out there to freeze regardless of what else was going on. By the way, it's the law. The law says I have to stop. *Everyone* has to stop. Doesn't mean anyone has to force you to accept help."

"But you kinda threatened it."

At that a small smile curved her lips. "I kinda did, didn't I?"

"Something about calling for backup. Gets attention every time."

"Got yours, I guess." Then she resumed pacing, still hugging herself. "I never saw a man so determined to kill his wife."

"That bad?"

She nodded shortly. "I've seen plenty of drunken fights. You can break them up, usually. The sound of racking a shotgun works pretty good. Failing that, a pistol shot into the ground. I've seen armed ranchers in a standoff ten feet apart over a stream arguing about who had water rights. That at least is a life-or-death problem, unlike a bar argument, but can usually be quieted without injury. But what happened the other night…" She shook her head and fell silent.

"What happened that night," she said eventually, "was pure evil and I was a part of it."

Then she turned her back. "I'm going to bed, Boyd. You need anything you know where to find it."

Boyd watched her disappear down the hall. A few minutes later he heard her showering. He hoped the heat helped ease the stiffness he'd seen in every part of her slender body.

After a bit he went to the kitchen to empty the beer bottle and rinse it in icy water. Leaving no trace of his passing. The lesson of long years in uniform.

Returning to the couch, the fire burning to embers in front of him, he looked into those dying flames that opened a door to memories he tried to avoid. Nights when he and his unit would have given almost anything to warm themselves by a fire. To sit around and shoot the breeze. The rare nights when they'd been able to, feeling like kings in their small, protected area.

Fire could mean a lot to a human. Everything. Warmth. Protection against wild animals. Hot food. Companionship. A barrier against the night. He'd never really thought about it until he'd been so often denied one.

Now here he was in a safe place, one where he could look into a fire and feel satisfied with life, just for this brief time. Reality always returned. Always. Usually with an explosion of bombs, grenades and bullets.

Or in this case an unwanted desire for Artie. A growing, strengthening need that made him despise himself. Hell, his timing sucked. He had to force his thoughts away from her curves and pretty face, her bright blue eyes, and return himself to the here and now.

There were those phone calls, which wouldn't leave him alone. He couldn't dismiss them the way Artie was.

In his experience bullies made threats. He was certain she was dismissing them as exactly that, and she might be right. But then there were those who enjoyed playing cat-and-mouse with only one ending for the mouse.

Not simply bullies full of big talk. There was never a way to be certain which kind you were dealing with, not until they gave themselves away through action or inaction.

He closed his eyes briefly, considering the kind of mind that would want to threaten Artie in the middle of a blizzard that had this entire county frozen like a Christmas display.

Just threats, but headed where? To accomplish what? He wished he'd gotten more information from Artie about the content of the calls. Some little bit might give away the entire show.

Then there was Artie's determination not to involve her colleagues. Stretched to breaking by the storm? Yeah. Maybe thinly spread over a county this size. But if she thought they wouldn't care... Well, she was wrong about that. They might not be able to put a guard on her house. Hell, at this point that wasn't even necessary. Artie was her own guard.

But what about trying to trace any of those calls? Find the originating cell tower or landline? He had no idea how long that might take, but did it matter if they put a lid on this?

Because Artie sure as hell didn't need this crap in her life.

He closed his eyes briefly, watching the flickering orange light through his eyelids. Fire. Sometimes it surrounded everyone's life, emotionally or in reality.

So she had experienced evil? He suspected that was a strong word for Artie to use. She had to have seen an awful lot as a cop, but this case had cut her to her core. It followed her even when she was trying to think of something else. He watched the flicker of pain or distress pass over her face even when she wasn't worrying about her father.

Evil. It had touched her somehow and it wouldn't leave her alone. Was she trying to find a way to do penance just as he was?

Sometimes the only penance, he was beginning to discover, was learning the lesson, never doing it again.

But what could she possibly have done? She'd broken up a domestic violent enough that the sheriff wanted her to take some time, to talk to a psychologist.

But that meant she'd inflicted some violence herself, didn't it? Had she needed to shoot someone? That would seriously rattle most people, at least until they became used to it, unfortunately.

Getting nowhere at all, he finally banked the fire, then stretched out on the couch. Sleep came easily and quickly to someone who'd had to take advantage of every possibility to cadge some.

But that didn't mean he wasn't alert. His ears never turned off, not anymore.

But all that filled them was an endless wind nosing noisily around the house.

No human threat out there.

Yet.

Chapter Eight

The morning brought silence. The sky remained leaden, the temperature looked frosty enough to cause dogs to shiver in their front yards, but there was no wind. Maybe the lightest of breezes.

And gently falling snow. Evidently it wasn't over yet. Nearly, but not completely.

Eventually the silence was broken by the snowplow passing in front of the house, clearing the street yet again. No one had yet ventured out to shovel walks or driveways. No one moved a car.

The world was hushed with expectancy.

Herman ate his oatmeal. Boyd and Artie toasted the last of the bread he'd made.

"I'm going to the store," Boyd announced. "Give me a list. Get me a list from Clara, too."

Artie put her hand on her hip as she stood near the counter and shook her head. "It's not over. The whiteout could whip up again."

"I'll manage. If not, you'll be free of an unwanted boarder."

"Damn it, Boyd!"

He shook his head and managed a crooked smile. "I've made my way through worse and you know it. Now get me those lists. And don't let Clara cheat, okay? Not every day someone gets a willing mule."

Twenty minutes later he had two lists tucked into the pocket of his arctic jacket, his empty backpack settled into place, and then headed out the front door.

God, the air smelled clean, with that particular scent that could come only from fresh snow.

No one was out and about except one man walking a Belgian Malinois who had black booties on his feet. They both looked as if the weather offered them no surprises.

The man's upright stride and the dog's attention told a story, Boyd thought. He paused, eyeing man and dog.

"Military?" he asked.

"Marines. Kell McLaren. This is Bradley, retired K-9."

Boyd thrust out a gloved hand. "Boyd Connor, retired Army, no K-9, sadly."

McLaren laughed and shook his hand. "Good to meet you. Staying awhile?"

"The storm got me thrust into Artie Jackson's house. No room at the inn and she took me in."

Kell nodded. "She's that kind of woman. Where are you off to?"

"The grocery. I need to replace some supplies. I'm hoping they're open."

"Open but not busy. Not sure how much is still on the shelves."

"Maybe my luck will hold." Then he paused, knowing he was probably breaking Artie's confidence but feeling the need to anyway. "Do you know if anyone might have a serious grudge against Artie?"

Kell McLaren stiffened, almost invisibly. "You got a concern?"

Boyd shook his head. "Just something she said."

"Well, a cop is going to have a lot of grudges against her, isn't she? People she arrested, helped put behind bars. It'd be weird if no one bore a grudge."

"Makes sense."

Kell nodded, but his gaze remained sharp. "Let me know if there's a worry. Give me your phone and I'll put my number on it."

Once the transaction was completed, Boyd moved on.

Well, that encounter had made him feel a bit better, Boyd thought as he resumed his hike toward the store. But then, so did being out in the air, on the move. Being on the move had been part of him for a long time.

And he liked that marine. Liked the way he appeared to believe that a military man might have a decent reason for a sixth sense operating overtime. Yeah, a good man.

Then he continued his trudge, trying to stop the images of Artie that persisted in bugging him. Damn, she was too attractive for his own good, and he had no place in his life for that now. Sure as hell not when the only place he wanted to be was in Seattle with Linda. Hiking toward some kind of healing with Linda.

Now he was trekking emotionally away from Artie. Hell.

THE HOUSE, Artie realized, felt surprisingly empty with Boyd gone. Not that he left much of a footprint, but his absence was more than that. A loneliness she'd never felt there before, except for a year or so after her mother died.

She sat with her dad before the fire that Boyd had conscientiously built early that morning.

"That man," Herman announced, "is going to burn through the entire winter's store of wood."

Artie laughed quietly. "So? I can get more from Jimmy."

"Yeah, I know. Long as we don't get caught in another blizzard that takes out the power before he gets another cord here."

Artie shook her head. "Come on, Dad, you know we have plenty out there already. Some of it's been there for years we burn it so rarely. But if you want to worry about it, I'll get Jimmy to deliver as soon as he can get here."

Herman waved an impatient hand. "Just being a grumpy old man and you know it. I always liked sitting in front of a fire with your mom."

Artie felt her heart clench. "Should I put it out?"

He nearly glared at her. "And take away that memory, too? I'm losing enough of them. It's a good memory. Let me have it."

How was she supposed to take that? Did he blame her for his memory losses? The idea that he might terrified her. She didn't know whether to apologize, so she left the subject alone. "What do you think of Boyd?" she asked after a while.

"If you had to drag in a stray, you couldn't have done better. Fine man, I believe, but dogged by something bad. Nothing he did, I don't think, but something sure has him unhappy as hell."

"Seems that way to me, too, Dad."

Herman nodded slowly. "Don't let him run off too soon, hear? Might be good for you to have someone around who doesn't have one foot in a grave."

"Dad!" Artie was appalled and jumped to her feet. "Dad! Don't say that!"

His gaze sharpened as he met hers. "It doesn't do any good to deny what we both know. I see you worrying all the time and I'm sorry I'm causing it. But it's the truth, Artie, and you can't keep trying to evade it, especially with me."

"I haven't been evading it," she said quietly, refusing the description. Wasn't she dealing with the situation day in and out? There was no evasion possible.

But her father disagreed. "Yes, you have. You won't talk about it with me. You watch my every mistake, my every sign I'm better, as if that's going to change a damn thing. You're living on tenterhooks because of me, swinging from hope to despair."

Artie's throat tightened until it hurt.

Her father continued, "You know, I'd kinda like to be able to talk frankly to you about it all. Not hide it so I don't upset you."

Artie's breathing became labored, shaky, as she took the punch of his words right in her solar plexus. "Dad…" she said weakly, then nearly ran into the kitchen where she gripped the edge of the counter and leaned over the sink as huge tears began to roll down her cheeks.

Dad. Oh, God, Daddy.

THE WIND RETURNED as Boyd walked to Artie's house. His backpack was full, and he carried several plastic bags, as well.

As the wind kicked up, visibility diminished. His balaclava didn't exactly do a great job, either, as it blew icy crystals into his face until his eyelashes were weighted with ice and his body chilled rapidly from every cold breath he drew.

He knew it all. He was used to it from the past. That didn't mean he liked it.

He entered Artie's house with his load and noted that Herman was sitting by himself in his recliner. No TV, just a small fire before him. And the Christmas tree, a tree that had at first given the man so much pleasure but now appeared all but invisible to him.

Cussing under his breath, Boyd headed for the kitchen and found Artie standing by herself, looking out the window at a world that had began to spin itself into another whiteout.

"How was it?" she asked. Her voice sounded thick, as if she'd been crying. Not that she'd ever want him to know that.

He started unloading onto the table. "The store wasn't terribly empty. They must have prepared, too. Anyway, I got everything on your list. If you want to start putting things away, I'll take Clara's over to her."

Artie nodded, keeping the back of her head to him.

He hesitated, then decided to just shut up. The woman rarely spoke about anything unless she chose to. It certainly wouldn't help anything to prod her when she was clearly already disturbed.

"Back in a few," he said after he gathered Clara's items in a plastic bag. "Which house?"

Artie pointed in the general direction.

Then back out into an increasingly ugly day. God, this weather ought to break soon, shouldn't it? A little bit of sunlight and maybe some quieter air would sure be welcome.

Clara Bateman must have been watching from her window. She opened the front door before he'd barely kicked the snow off his boots.

"You must be Boyd," she greeted him warmly. "Come in. I can't thank you enough for going to the grocery for me."

Boyd managed a smile. "I was going out for a walk anyway."

"Hate being cooped up?"

"Believe it."

She led the way into her warm, bright kitchen. When he'd placed the bags on her table, she looked through them. "I think," she said dryly, "that you brought me some things that weren't on my list."

"Everybody deserves a treat. I just hope you're not diabetic."

She laughed. "I missed that, thank goodness. Tea? Coffee?"

He might have accepted. This cheery, plump woman, with a thatch of gray hair that looked as if it never took orders from a brush, was inviting. Warm. Bright. Unlike the gloom in the Jackson house. But he understood the gloom over there and didn't expect the Jacksons to put on some kind of performance for him. Especially since he was an invader.

Besides, he was worried about Artie, about her mood when he returned from the store. He shook his head at himself. She didn't need *him* to get her through a day. Clearly she stood on her own two feet.

But that didn't prevent him from worrying. Besides, welcome as Clara's cheer might be, the darkness inside him wouldn't yield to it for long.

"How's the old man doing?" Clara asked as she put the Danish on the counter. "Do you have any idea how long it's been since I treated myself to a pastry?"

"Of course I don't." He summoned a smile. "You're talking about Herman, I gather."

"Yeah, that old man. The only one I worry about. You aren't getting to see much of it, but we have some great times, him and me."

"Been friends for a long time?"

"Most of our lives. Both of us even married our high school sweethearts. Don't hear much of that these days, do you?"

"I wouldn't know. High school was a long time ago."

She flashed him a smile. "For all of us." Then she eyed him. "You want to run, don't you? Won't even sit for a minute."

He opened his mouth to apologize, but Clara forestalled him. "I'm not offended, Boyd. You get on back and tell Herman I'm going to beat him at dominoes the next time I come over."

"Will do." Boyd straightened and pulled his balaclava down again, wet from melted snow and his breath. Good thing it was wool.

"And, Boyd?" Clara said as he turned to go.

"Yeah?"

"Look after Artie as much as she'll let you. I swear she refuses help almost like it's an insult. Anyway, you don't much know her, being here only a short time, but please do what you can."

He nodded. "I can promise that, Clara."

He was a man who kept his promises, even when they conflicted and he had to balance them out. But he kept them.

ARTIE HAD UNPACKED the groceries by the time Boyd returned. He'd gone beyond her small list, too, bringing home some sugary treats that were sure to please Herman. More packets of cocoa. More canned soups. He'd not only replaced whatever they'd used while he was there but had brought enough to make sure they were stocked up for a while to come.

Was he planning to stay? She was nearly appalled to realize that she hoped he would. But then she remembered the wanderer, the man who said his destination was the next mile. No, he'd move on as soon as he could.

"Hi, Herman," she heard him say in the next room. "Clara says she's going to beat you at dominoes next time she comes over."

Herman laughed. "She always says that. Rarely does."

Artie smiled faintly. She was fairly certain her dad was exaggerating.

She hesitated to join the two men, though. The sting from what her father had said remained with her. Worse, it was one of those instants that changed her self-perception completely. An emotional whiplash.

Like what had happened at the Lauers'. Man, she was trying hard not to think about that. Could an effort to avoid thinking about something become physically exhausting?

Then her phone rang. She froze.

AT HOME, the Lathrop brothers discovered that their landline once again functioned. The first thing they did was get on the horn with Mack Murdo, their friend in just about everything.

Mack's voice poured out of their speakerphone. "Look," Mack said roughly, "you gotta be careful 'bout calling me. It's not like I can get out of this here house right now. The woman and them brats is all over. A man can't get no privacy."

"We still gotta do something more to scare that woman off," Willie argued. "Can't let this go on till she sends Billy or Joe up."

Mack growled. "Didn't help my DUI none. Didn't need no cop." Through the phone came the shrieking of kids in the background. "Damn it," Mack swore. "You ain't been listening!"

Joe hammered his hand on the arm of his chair.

The beating he'd given it over the years had fractured some of it and now it drove a large splinter into the palm of his hand. Joe jumped up, cussing loudly and kicking at the door frame, which only made two toes hurt like hell.

The dogs of the world, wherever they were, would be grateful that the Lathrops had never wanted one of them. Damn dogs were too much trouble, always needing somethin'.

"Just shut the hell up," Willie growled. "You freakin' fool, hurtin' yourself. Can't talk to Mack with you shoutin' yer fool head off."

Joe shut up, then hunted for a pair of pliers to pull out the splinter. It hurt coming out, but the drops of blood afterward gave him an excuse to suck on it. He'd always liked the taste.

"Okay," Mack said. "Can you listen now? I told you what that damn fool lawyer told me, if'n I can remember exac'ly. Said they had me because of a blood test and the camera on the damn cop car. Told me not to fight cuz they might get harder on me. As if takin' my license twern't bad enough, but least tain't jail."

"Yeah, yeah," Willie answered. "We heard all that. But we ain't talking about you. You keep sayin' it's bad if that damn cop testifies. We gonna scare her off with the calls."

Mack growled. "Keepin' you from being more stupid is all them calls do."

"Hey, it was your idea."

Mack snorted. "I didn't say to keep it up. My cousin, the lawyer in Gillette?"

"The one who works all them fancy deals for the oil companies. Yeah. Crooked like all of 'em."

Mack didn't argue the point. Seemed obvious to all of them anyway. Lawyers were crooked.

"Like I was sayin'," Mack said, lowering his voice. "God dang it, hang on. I gotta get into the garage afore the rug rats drive me nuts. And Marilou's ears be flapping around listening."

The Lathrop brothers waited, hearing doors slam. Hearing the wind blow into the phone's speaker, hearing another, heavier slam.

"Damn it all to hell," Mack said finally. "Put me in mind why I didn't never get that space heater out here?"

"Fire," answered Joe promptly. "You was worried about all that old dust."

"I *know* that," Mack snapped.

"Then why…"

Willie spoke. "Shut up, Joe. That was one of them questions that ya don't answer."

"Oh." Joe went back to nursing his hand.

"Anyways," Mack said, after a loud cough, "my cousin says you either gotta deal or go to court. You wanna deal for a manslaughter charge, Joe? You at least got a chance for that, just a brawl is all. Gonna be worse for Billy, mark my words. I hear he banged up that woman of his pretty bad. Near killed her. You ain't likely gonna get a bargain on that."

Willie froze. "You asked him about *us*? You let him know?"

"I told him I was asking about something I read.

He don't know this is for real. My feelin' is he don't *want* to know nohow."

Willie relaxed somewhat. "Okay."

"Anyway, he said they might deal on Joe cuz bar fights happen alla time and Joe didn't mean no harm, 'ceptin' to punch the guy. Ain't Joe's fault the bozo hit his head on the bar. Bad side of that is ever'body liked that damn cowboy and them prosecutors might decide not to deal. Anyhow, my cousin says they bargain that alla time, might this time. Mebbe. You gotta get 'em to bargain. Ain't gonna bargain Billy's case, though."

"Why the hell not?" Willie demanded.

"Headlines," Mack answered, voice heavy with inside knowledge. "Can't let headlines be that the effing state went easy on a guy who set about killin' his wife. My cousin says they'll take Billy all the way to court, and they's gonna need that damn deputy to do it. She's what my cousin said is the eyewitness. Somebody who saw it happen."

For a minute, the line crackled almost emptily.

"Meaning?" Joe asked finally, his hand forgotten.

"Meaning that bitch is gonna testify. She can't refuse. They can force her. Meaning Billy Lauer ain't got no excuses, 'ceptin' maybe that cop is blind."

More silence. Willie cleared his throat. "You sayin'?"

"You know exac'ly what I's saying. They got enough on Billy. Don't go makin' it worse by tryin' to stop that cop. They won't deal then, not with you, not with Billy."

Willie hung up with a slam. Like he was ever going to listen to that wimp Mack. "We're gonna call again."

"Mack was sayin' twouldn't be smart."

"Like I care."

Chapter Nine

When the phone rang again, the landline, Artie didn't want to answer it. Not this time. With the storm quieting down at last, this house didn't feel quite as secure as it had before.

It was now nearly accessible to a determined person.

For the first time, she couldn't just dismiss the threats. They were clinging to her back like cold, wet leaves even though they were so unlikely. But another one?

She could feel Boyd's gaze on her as she didn't reach for the phone. Did he think she was a coward? What did that matter? The worst thing about ignoring the call was that it might be the office. Someone who needed her.

She was just screwing herself up to reach for the damn thing when Herman called out, "Aren't you getting that, Artie? Your business phone I thought."

"Want me to get it?" Boyd asked almost inaudibly. He stood in the kitchen doorway.

"No." God, she was being an idiot and making herself look like a coward in front of a man who'd probably *never* been a coward. She reached for the receiver and said in a clipped tone, "Jackson."

Then she heard the ugly voice again, but this time ice ran down her spine. "You better forget," the voice said. "Forget ever'thin' you seen. Cuz I can *make* you forget. Or maybe you should be worrying about your old man."

Then the click of a disconnected line. Artie punched the buttons to call back, but only a beeping answered her. Nor would the punch buttons give her the caller's number.

God! She slammed the receiver onto the cradle and closed her eyes. A threat against her father. And what the hell was she supposed to forget?

"Artie?" Boyd had stepped closer.

She squeezed the words out. "Another threat. This time he mentioned my dad."

Boyd closed the distance between them and without asking wrapped her in his arms. Strong arms. She gripped his sides and let her head fall against his shoulder.

All of a sudden she didn't feel alone. This stranger no longer felt like a stranger. He had begun to feel like a friend.

"You don't need anyone telling you what to do," he murmured, holding her close.

Yeah, and she was grateful that he didn't try to tell her what she needed to do. Now that her dad had been threatened, she knew she could no longer ignore this bastard.

Reluctantly she freed herself from the surprisingly

welcome embrace and called the office number. Guy Redwing answered immediately. "What's up, Artie?"

"Sheesh, are you guys still bedded down there?"

"Might be getting some relief later today, if the weather keeps improving. So, you have a problem?"

"Threatening phone calls. Four of them now, and this one mentioned my father. Can you track the calls to my landline and cell? Find out, maybe, where they're coming from?"

"You got it," Guy answered, suddenly sounding all business. "You want someone to keep watch at your place?"

"You guys are already understaffed and over-worked. I can protect myself and my dad. Other people are gonna need you more after this storm."

"Your call," Guy answered, but he didn't sound pleased. "You let us know if anything at all happens, including another call. Got it?"

"Got it. And, Guy? Somehow my landline number got out there. I've kept it private for official use only."

Guy swore. "You better believe I'm gonna look into that."

When Artie hung up, she felt marginally better. Marginally.

"Think they can locate the numbers?" Boyd asked.

She turned to face him. "I don't know. The cells can be tracked to a nearby tower but given all the wide-open space out there, cell towers haven't sprouted like weeds. Satellite phones are more useful but I don't know about tracking them. Then there's the possibility of pay-as-you-go phones. Might not be registered to a real person. Guy might do better with the landline."

He nodded.

She started to walk past him, to go put her eyes on her father and ensure herself he was still there, still okay. That call had seriously set her on edge.

Boyd spoke before she'd moved two feet. "Maybe you don't want it, but I can help. I used to be pretty good at what I did."

She didn't need a road map to understand that he referred to his Army experience. To his combat experience.

She looked at him again with fresh eyes. This time she saw a strong, tall and determined man with a square face chiseled by weather. A face that right now seemed to have a hard edge.

He might be hiking to nowhere, but she had no doubt he'd know how to help defend her father.

Which, in the end, was all that mattered.

STILL NO SUN to melt the top layer of snow. Still gray clouds that continued to sift down new flakes. Still occasional gusts that whitened the world.

To hell with it. Boyd went hunting in Artie's small shed and emerged with a snow shovel. He passed through the house with it after kicking off the snow from his boots in the mudroom.

"You and Herman be okay if I go shovel some? Clara needs to be able to get help if she gets sick and as far as I can tell the plow has been dumping a lot of snow on the edge of walkways and driveways."

"We'll be fine," Artie answered, bristling.

He liked the sight of that bristling and smiled. "Figured you would, but asking is polite. Besides, I'll have my eyes on the surrounding area. In case."

She answered dryly, "Whenever you can see, that is."

"There is that."

Outside, though, felt like momentary freedom. If there was one thing he'd learned about himself during his long trek, it was that he no longer found the outdoors to be threatening, like during the war. No, now he felt the expansive beauty of it all.

Thanks to the leaden sky, twilight was settling in earlier than usual. He headed directly for Clara's place, determined that if she needed help an ambulance stretcher would be able to get to her door.

The work felt good to nearly every muscle in his body. He wasn't used to being as inactive as he'd been the past few days.

The snowbank along the street in front of Clara's house and driveway was hard-packed and heavy. At least he felt as if he were accomplishing something with each heft of the shovel. Using his muscles felt good, but the cold was getting to his injured knee, stiffening it, bringing the pain to the fore. He ignored it.

He kept scanning the area, too. Few people were emerging, although he saw a guy a few houses down tackling the snow. Someone else walked a dog in the front yard, leaving a yellow stain behind. He tossed a friendly wave in their direction. Life moving on again, bit by bit.

He ought to be moving on, too. Dealing with the realities he might have faced during his last call with Shelley. Was she really trying to keep him from Linda? Or was Linda so estranged from him she just didn't want to see him? Especially not during this time when men must all appear awful to her.

He shook his head, scattering the useless wondering, and kept on with the snow. By the time he reached Clara's porch the snow had become lighter, drier. The wind might undo every bit of his work along the walk to her porch. He mentally shrugged. Then he'd just do it again.

Clara appeared briefly to thank him and offer him a hot drink, but he shook his head. "You just get inside and stay warm. I gotta get on to Artie's house."

More heavy labor, every bit of it making his body happy. The rest of him not so much. He *had* to find a way to stay here, especially since a threat had been made to Herman. Artie probably *could* take care of herself, but her father at the same time? It could turn into a real mess.

Maybe he could use Shelley as his excuse for not moving on right away. She was sure a damn good excuse for a lot, including some of the disappointment he felt for himself. Some of the self-hatred. He hadn't built that pile entirely on his own, although he was only just beginning to admit it to himself. No, the poisoning hadn't started with his PTSD. It had started earlier in their marriage.

Not everyone was cut out to be a military wife.

FROM HER FRONT WINDOW, Artie watched Boyd perform the yeoman's work of clearing all that snow. He was being generous doing Clara's walk and driveway, too. Hell, at the rate he was going he might do more of her neighbors' houses, as well.

Except the twilight had abandoned the sky. The only light now was reflected off the snow by the street-lights and some coming through windows of houses. Everyone but Boyd had disappeared inside.

At last Boyd reached her porch, shoveled a bit more, then stomped his way around to the back of the house with the shovel. To return it to the shed. To enter through the mudroom. Always considerate.

Then she went back to her dad who was now play-ing checkers with himself. It had always amused her that he could play both sides objectively, mainly be-cause, as he always said, he didn't care which side won.

For a lot of years, though, he and Artie's mom had played checkers together. And dominoes. Neither had seemed especially interested in card games although they played them from time to time. When they did, they placed bets with paper clips.

"Dad?"

He looked up. "Wanna play?"

Artie shook her head. "No. I just suddenly won-dered why we never got another dog after Maple died." A thought that had sprung out of nowhere, catching her by surprise.

Herman's face saddened. "Your mom couldn't bear the thought. Just couldn't. Losing animals is hard, Artie."

Artie nodded, accepting it as fact. She'd seen her friends grieve after they lost a pet but somehow apologetically, as if they felt it shouldn't be as big a deal as losing a family member.

For some, she would have guessed, it was every bit as bad. She sure had grieved for Maple, even as a small child.

"Why'd you ask?"

"Just crossed my mind. Who knows why?" Except she suddenly knew why. A dog on alert would have been a comfort right now. To hear barks of warning.

But there was no dog. And she realized she was relying on a man who really *was* a stranger. A few days and a glimpse of his war service didn't change that.

Yet his presence had begun to comfort her.

Man, she was a mess. Thoughts of the Lauer incident kept pressing at the corners of her mind, demanding attention. Attention she couldn't afford to give it right now.

Maybe that psychologist would be a good thing after all.

OUTSIDE, HEADED FOR the shed, in the very dim light where only streetlamps bouncing back off snow gave any light at all, Boyd stopped dead in his tracks.

Those darker shadows in the snow were footprints. And they weren't his.

Someone had been out here. Not to go to the shed as he had. He could still see his own prints clearly. Straight from the shed to the mudroom. These went crossways, as if someone had walked along the back of the house.

Seeking a way in? Moving close enough to the house where the snow hadn't become as deep thanks to escaping heat. Where the crust had begun to build, making the prints as clear as if they were stamped there.

He put the shovel in the shed, then went to follow the footprints. Easy to see they had come from the yard next door. Had passed right behind Artie's house, then continued toward the alley behind the house.

Who the hell would be walking there?

He looked sharply around, knowing it was too late to see anyone, but needing to look anyway. He followed the prints to the alley, then lost them. Snow several feet deep had blown into the narrow alley, obliterating everything.

Any hope that Artie might cherish about this all being empty, bullying threats had just vanished.

Someone wanted her badly enough to come out in this weather and get near her house. Maybe scoping the place out.

Hell.

Chapter Ten

Knowing Boyd had been out in the cold for a couple of hours, knowing someone had to do it, Artie cooked dinner. They all needed to eat, Boyd most of all.

The need didn't change her feelings about cooking. She sometimes wondered why she hated it so much, then always thought about her mother. Mom had buzzed around in the kitchen a lot, making it her domain, always in the midst of preparing something delicious.

A life as far away as any Artie had wanted for herself. She'd never wanted to be a housewife, or anything approaching it. Cooking must symbolize the worst of it for her, somehow.

At least the desire for a spotless house hadn't caused her a problem. No, cleaning was a good way to stay busy and it was something everyone needed to do, not just a housewife.

Or so she rationalized all of it.

Regardless, she cooked that night. A jar of marinara, browned hamburger, shredded mozzarella, ricotta and uncooked rotini with a couple of cups of water. All in one pan, simmered for a little less than half an hour. The rotini came out cooked, the meal cheesy and thick.

Where the heck had she learned that from? Mom, of course. In some distant recess of her memory, she'd recalled this dish. Amazingly enough, she even had the cheese.

But Boyd had been shopping. If he had plans for some of this food bursting out of her fridge and pantry, he was out of luck now.

Distraction. Cooking at least provided some. Distraction from the Lauer incident, distraction from the phone calls.

The threat against her father. God in heaven, who would do that? What reason could there be?

While dinner simmered, while she heard Boyd come back in through the mudroom, she gripped the edge of the counter and stared out into the blackness of the window over the kitchen sink.

All her life she'd liked the night. Until now. Now it loomed, pressing in against the glass. Full of threat.

"That smells good," Boyd said as he entered the kitchen. The night's cold entered with him.

Before she could summon some kind of response, the kitchen phone rang again. She exploded.

"Damn it! Damn it, damn it, damn it!" Someone kept walking into her house through that damn phone connection. They might as well have entered through the front door. Worse, they came with a threat.

"I'll get it," Boyd said before she could move.

She wanted to stop him. It was *her* phone, *her* problem. But he'd already reached for the receiver.

"Hello," he said, his voice level.

After a moment, he turned and handed her the phone. "Gage Dalton. The sheriff, he said?"

Relieved, so relieved that Artie's legs momentarily weakened, she took the phone from him.

"Hi, Gage," she said, her voice fairly steady.

"Who the hell just answered your phone, Artie? That wasn't your father."

"Uh, no." Lord, how to explain this in less than a thousand words? And to Gage, who parented his deputies as if they were his own family?

"Artie," Gage said. Just her name. Letting her know he wouldn't let her off the hook.

"It's Boyd Connor. When I was coming back from the Lauer incident, I found him walking along the road. The storm was just beginning. The motel is full. So he's staying with me."

Gage fell briefly silent. "This is the man you had Guy do a background on?"

"Yes. He's clean."

"And when did those phone calls start?"

There it was again, the suspicion. Except that Boyd had been standing right there when some of those calls came. "It wasn't him. He was right here."

Gage again fell silent. "I'm going to come over. Be there in an hour or so."

"The roads…"

Gage's answer was dry. "It's been a very long time since I worked out of Miami. I'm pretty sure I've learned to handle these winter roads."

She replaced the receiver on the hook and looked

at Boyd. "Sounds like you're going to get interrogated before long. We'd better eat before it gets cold."

If Boyd felt one way or another about Gage coming over to question him, he showed it in no way. But then Boyd could become amazingly impassive sometimes.

Herman shuffled in from the living room, a smile on his face. "Smells like something your mother used to make."

"I think it is." And Herman was still in the present, a good thing. Some of Artie's tightening tension eased. Too much, she thought. Sometimes it all felt like too much, and since Billy Lauer, that feeling had become stronger than ever.

Herman was in a good mood. He chatted throughout dinner, telling a few of his well-worn jokes, all of which appeared to entertain Boyd. Or maybe Boyd was just being polite.

Hard to know at this point. But she remembered his embrace earlier and she knew for certain that his hug hadn't been merely polite. He'd been offering genuine comfort insofar as she would let him.

Maybe her dad was right about her when he sometimes said she was a prickly pear cactus. What had made her that way?

Damned if she knew or cared. Just being herself had always been important to her.

Except she was beginning to wonder if she was becoming a train wreck.

Lauer. Her thoughts kept returning to that beast, much as she tried to bury him. Returning to his savagery. To her own. Losing her self-control. Beating a man with every ounce of strength in her body.

She didn't much like that Artie Jackson.

GAGE TURNED UP just after the last dish had been washed, while a fresh pot of coffee was brewing. As usual, Gage wanted the coffee. Sometimes Artie thought he lived on it.

He settled onto the couch, his smile crooked because of the burned and grafted skin on the side of his face. The man winced nearly every time he moved, limped with nearly every step, and never once complained. He'd been crippled by a car bomb that had killed his first family but had learned to live with it all.

Artie frankly admired him.

Boyd leaned against the wall, arms folded, wearing his gray sweats again, leaving room on the recliners and couch for the other three. Herman looked pleased to have company, and he'd always liked Gage.

Sipping coffee from his mug, Gage looked at Artie. "Got the report on Bea Lauer."

Artie drew a sharp breath. Her last image of that woman was of her lying in a pool of her own blood while her husband tried to strangle her. Too vivid. "How is she?"

"She's going to survive. Physically anyway. Emotionally is another thing."

Artie nodded, staring down into her own cup, drawing in the aroma of coffee, seeking to hold at bay all the terrible feelings that were trying to flood her. "She's going to have to overcome a whole lot."

"Years of abuse, I hear. One of those situations we don't hear about until it's almost too late. Or already too late."

"I can't disagree." But Artie was tensing again with a different concern, waiting for Gage's inquisition of Boyd. Maybe she'd learn more about him. Or maybe she'd discover he had something important to hide.

But Gage didn't turn immediately to Boyd. He wasn't done with Artie yet. "So how'd you get a stranger in your house?"

"I told you."

Gage nodded thoughtfully. "Coulda put him in an unlocked holding cell."

Boyd interrupted, "Given her description of one of those holding cells versus her house, when she offered her house I took it."

Gage's dark gaze settled on him. "Risky, maybe?"

"Risky for who? *I* knew I wouldn't hurt her. As for what she said when I pointed out that taking me home with her could be dangerous…" Boyd shrugged. "She said she was a cop, she had a gun, a baton and tae kwon do. That I'd get more than I bargained for if I gave her any trouble."

Gage astonished Artie with a loud laugh. "That's Artie, all right. But all that protection might not have been enough against you, would it?"

"Probably not."

Gage offered another one of his crooked smiles. "Military, I hear."

"Army."

"Four tours in Afghanistan."

Boyd leaned forward, settling his elbows on his knees. "Yeah." His face had darkened a bit.

He wasn't liking this direction in the conversation, Artie thought. But why?

"A nice set of medals," Gage continued. "A hero, I guess."

Boyd shook his head. "No hero." Then he straightened a bit. "My military record is no secret. You want to know something else, so ask it."

"I want to know what you're doing walking through my county, nearly two thousand miles from your last known address, in the dead of winter with nothing but a pack on your back."

Oh, wow, Artie thought. Now she was wound tighter than a drum skin, her hands clenched around her coffee mug. How would Boyd respond to that? The insinuation was there, however subtle: Boyd must be up to no good.

She realized she was chewing her lower lip and forced herself to stop. She glanced at her dad and found him intensely focused on what was happening in his living room. As welcoming as he had been to Boyd, evidently he had some doubts of his own. Some doubts that probably revolved around his daughter's safety.

Was everyone in this room thinking she must be some kind of fool? She'd wondered that initially when she brought Boyd home, but the wondering hadn't lasted long. Her only excuse for offering him shelter in her own home had to do with her own mental and

"One Minute" Survey

GET YOUR FREE BOOKS AND A FREE GIFT!

✓ Complete this Survey   ✓ Return this survey

1 Do you try to find time to read every day?
☐ YES   ☐ NO

2 Do you prefer stories with suspensful storylines?
☐ YES   ☐ NO

3 Do you enjoy having books delivered to your home?
☐ YES   ☐ NO

4 Do you share your favorite books with friends?
☐ YES   ☐ NO

YES! I have completed the above "One Minute" Survey. Please send me m
Free Books and a Free Mystery Gift (worth over $20 retail). I understand that I am
under no obligation to buy anything, as explained on the back of this card.

☐ **Harlequin® Romantic Suspense**
240/340 CTI G2AD

☐ **Harlequin Intrigue® Larger-Print**
199/399 CTI G2AD

☐ **BOTH**
240/340 & 199/399
CTI G2AE

FIRST NAME

LAST NAME

ADDRESS

APT.#   CITY

STATE/PROV.   ZIP/POSTAL CODE

EMAIL ☐ Please check this box if you would like to receive newsletters and promotional emails from
Harlequin Enterprises ULC and its affiliates. You can unsubscribe anytime.

HI/HRS-1123-OM

emotional state after Billy Lauer. A lousy excuse if ever there was one.

She wasn't one to defend her choices, though. She made them and lived with them. Like Billy Lauer. Sometimes it was harder than other times, though.

"You gonna answer my question?" Gage asked after a pregnant pause.

Boyd shook his head slightly. "How much do you really need to know, Sheriff?"

"Start with why you quit your construction job after only two months."

Artie caught her breath. Gage sure wasn't pulling any punches.

Boyd's mouth tightened. "Family emergency."

Gage lifted the one eyebrow that was still mobile. "How much of an emergency when you're walking across the country? I hear planes are faster these days."

Boyd unfolded his arms but remained relaxed. At least on the surface. Artie thought she saw something hard glitter in his eyes.

"I don't know how much you think you have a right to know about my personal situation, Sheriff."

"Just enough to know you aren't trouble on the hoof."

Boyd looked down, drawing a deep breath. When he raised his face it hinted at sorrow. "Some families get broken pretty badly. So do some vets. I'm walking off a lot of personal trouble."

That seemed to satisfy Gage. It only whetted Artie's curiosity. She wanted to know the story behind this trek of Boyd's. She wanted to fill in all the blanks. But, like Gage, she had no right to anything Boyd didn't want to share.

Unable to hold still any longer, she went to get the coffeepot and freshen mugs.

Herman spoke for the first time. "Seems to me like there's a lot of problems a man's got to work out on his own. By himself."

Boyd nodded faintly. Gage settled back a bit on the couch, wincing as he did so. He gulped more coffee.

"Now," he said, facing Artie, "I want to know more about these phone calls."

Artie immediately glanced at her dad. She didn't want him to know about any of this. Gage followed her gaze and gave a brief nod as if to himself. "Alrighty, then. I'll just finish this coffee, if you don't mind, Artie, then I'll be on my way. And Guy's running down those calls for you, okay?"

"Thanks." Artie was surprised by how much gratitude she felt. It was as if her colleagues were steadily closing ranks around her. Like Gage coming over here on icy streets to check up on the situation.

Even though she kept insisting she was fine, that she could take care of herself, she couldn't deny that it was comforting to know she wasn't facing this all alone.

HER DAD WENT to bed shortly after Gage departed. Once tucked in, he opted to turn on his bedroom TV, this time to a movie, some kind of drama. The kind of movie her mother had preferred. Sound and motion to block him off from the rest of the world, maybe from his memories. Or maybe a deep dive into them.

Artie felt another wave of sorrow. Herman had lost his wife and now he was losing himself, piece by piece. Could anything be more awful?

Well, it could: someone hurting him to get even with her about something she couldn't begin to imagine. What had that guy meant by telling her to forget? Forget what?

Her spine stiffened and by the time she settled in her recliner, she was beginning to feel very angry. Some sicko was forcing his way into her life, threatening her father. For the first time in her life, she actually *wanted* to use her baton, and would if anyone broke in here.

Boyd sat on the couch, leaning back, legs casually crossed. "What's going on?" he asked eventually.

"About what?" She was in no mood to be questioned, or to feel obligated to answer those questions.

"The threats. Any ideas?"

"None. Too opaque, too general." She put her chin in her hand and had to admit she liked Boyd's attention to the fire. It was more soothing than a blast of central heat, more relaxing by far.

"But your father? Does Gage know that?"

"He picked up on it, didn't you see?" She shook her head. "Gage misses almost nothing."

"I've been worried Herman might be at risk since you told me about the first call."

She turned her head, scowling at him. "You think that didn't cross my mind? Now it's overt."

Then she had a feeling. A strange feeling that seemed to come out of nowhere. Her entire attention focused on Boyd. "You know something and you'd better tell me."

His lips compressed and he appeared to be preparing to tell her nothing at all. Finally he said, "I don't lie. Unfortunately."

"Except by omission, evidently. So what are you omitting?"

His frown deepened. "When I went to put the shovel back in the shed, I saw footprints. Walking close to the back of your house, headed for the alley. They disappeared there. The snow must have blown over them."

Artie rose from her seat, anger starting to burn in the pit of her stomach. "You didn't think I needed to know this?"

"I think I didn't have a time to tell you, Artie. Damn it, it's not as if we're hiding ourselves away in some private part of the house. You wanted me to say this in front of Herman?"

Her anger seeped away like the air from a punctured balloon. "God Almighty, this sucks."

"I'll second that." He rose, too, and began pacing the small living room. "I'm glad I'm here. You won't accept any backup from your department, so you're stuck with me. I'm your backup."

She wrapped her arms around herself as if trying to ease a deep chill. Her legs were planted firmly, however. The fight in her was far from gone.

"I don't need backup." But she didn't sound quite as certain as she had when all this started.

"Maybe *you* don't," he said evenly. "But what about

Herman? Sounds like you're going to need an extra fist in this house."

She liked the way Boyd phrased that. Not as if she needed protecting, but as if she might need help protecting both herself and her father.

As well she might.

Then Boyd stopped pacing in front of her. "What's Gage's story? It must be a bad one from the look of him."

She nodded, trying to uncoil the tension in her neck, her back. Tension that hadn't left her since Lauer.

"He used to be undercover with DEA. A car bomb killed his family and nearly killed him, as well."

"My God," Boyd murmured.

"Yeah. I admire the hell out of that man."

"I can see why."

Then Artie pinned him with her gaze. "So what's *your* story, Boyd? Not just the bits and pieces."

Chapter Eleven

Willie was still trying to warm up in front of the fire, practically sitting on top of it. "Gotta get a better parka soon." Then he waved away the cold beer Joe tried to hand him.

"For hell's sake, Joe, coffee. Ise freezin'!"

Joe hurried to obey, stacking the percolator and putting it on the hearth. It wasn't long before they could hear the bubble of the coffee perking.

"Booze is s'posed to warm ya," Joe said.

"Sure. Coffee does it better."

Joe didn't argue. Arguing with Willie when he was in a certain mood could be rightly dangerous. "So what'd you see?"

"A woman and her old man livin' in a house like we thought. One kink."

Joe didn't like the sound of kinks, even just one. "Yeah?"

"Got a man livin' with her. Don't know him, never seed him afore. Mebbe just because of the storm."

"He a problem?" Joe asked nervously.

"I dunno. He was out shoveling snow when I first

seed him." Willie shook his head and reached for the coffeepot, not caring if it had finished perking. "Point is, it don't matter."

"Why not?"

"Cuz they ain't much that can stand up against a gun."

Joe liked the sound of that. He began to smile.

But Willie never left Joe very happy for long. "Been thinkin' though."

"Bout what?"

"Looked easier afore this storm. Now that damn cop is stuck to her house like glue. We gotta get her away from there."

"Why?"

"Damn it, Joe, whatsa matter with your brain? You wanna leave evidence all over that house?"

Joe felt unhappy again. "This is gettin' harder."

"Never was gonna be easy."

"But that was good, say'n about her dad. That's gotta scare her."

"Mebbe."

Willie returned to brooding and Joe wisely shut up. Whatever Willie said, it *was* getting harder. The easy plan they'd started with, of scaring that cop off, was springing up problems like weeds. Like them damn dandelions that showed up every spring.

MORE COFFEE. Boyd made the pot. They settled at the kitchen table for some reason. Maybe because it was less comfortable, suited for a difficult conversation. Or maybe because it was farther from Herman. Artie had a strong feeling neither of them wanted this story to be overheard.

Artie waited, but when Boyd didn't speak, she looked into his tight face and said, "Well? Gage was right, this hike of yours doesn't sound like a family emergency."

"It is." He wiped his hand over his face, calluses scratching a bit on the day's stubble. "Except I can't do a damn thing about any of it."

"Except walk?"

"Walk and wait." He turned his face away a bit, staring at something only he could see. "I don't talk about this."

"You told me once it could be helpful to talk." Except tossing his words back at him seemed a little harsh on her part. Seemed too pushy, although she believed she had a justifiable need to know more about Boyd Connor.

"About some things. Not everything." He fell silent again.

And once again, Artie waited. Some things couldn't be pushed. No way. Some things had to come in their own good time. At least now he seemed willing to talk, a little anyway. So she waited.

Eventually Boyd spoke again. "I made a hash of my life, I'm a huge failure, and now I'm wondering if my ex will ever let me see my daughter again. She was supposed to, but that last phone call with her…" He shook his head, allowing the words to trail off.

Artie felt her chest begin to tighten. This guy was

carrying more than a backpack. It sounded like a hell of a mess.

After a bit, Boyd's gaze returned to her. It was utterly naked, hiding nothing of his anguish. "I blew it, Artie. All of it. I lost my marriage, I guess I lost my daughter, I sometimes lose my mind, and if I got any angrier I'd be a cinder."

Artie didn't know how to reply. Any words that sprang to her mind seemed trivial. She didn't want to trivialize any part of what he was saying or feeling. Rightly or wrongly, this man must feel gutted.

The only thing she could do was reach across the table and rest her hand over his. To her great surprise, he turned his hand over and gripped her fingers gently. Warmth. Human touch. So very important. It felt good to her, too, bridging the gap she'd been trying to place between herself and the world. An important bridge.

"Tell me," she said quietly. She wasn't sure she wanted to hear this, but she needed to. Needed to better understand this man who had blown into her life on a blizzard and was now insisting he would stay to back her up. That meant he was caring, right? The way he treated her father, so kindly, as if Herman had no problem at all. And now he wanted to help look after both of them. That caring on his part called out the caring in her.

God, the two of them were a hot mess!

He rubbed his free hand over his face again, as if trying to wash something away. Then he spoke, his voice carrying an edge.

"I was in the Army, right? You know that. What you don't know is how rarely I was actually home. Shelley—my ex—didn't want to live anywhere near where I posted, so it wasn't like I could just drop in when I had a couple of days."

Artie blew a long breath. "Why didn't she want to live near your posts?" When she thought of being in love, she didn't imagine choosing to live apart, at least not for long. Was this weird or something?

"Her family," Boyd answered. "She wanted to be near them, to stay in the town where she had all her family and friends. Especially after she became pregnant with Linda, it made perfect sense to me."

"Sense maybe. But difficult anyway."

He shrugged one shoulder and looked at her again. "It was the way she wanted it. I could understand her not wanting to move to some strange place where I was the only person she knew. I thought it was best for her, too."

"Then?"

"Maybe not the best for the two of us. For our marriage. I came home when I could, but I wasn't exactly overwhelmed with free time. I got thirty days a year for leave, but it didn't always come in a huge block. Sometimes just a week or two, depending on my unit's orders."

Artie could already hear what was coming. The ache in her heart deepened a bit. "Did she ever come visit you?"

"A couple of times. She didn't like it, especially when Linda was small. I got it."

Artie bet he got it. Whatever had brought about the marriage in the first place evidently had begun vanishing quickly.

"Anyway," Boyd continued after a minute or so, "I was busy. It was the way things were and I didn't give it a lot of thought. Making Shelley happy, I thought. Only I wasn't. And I saw so little of my daughter I'm honestly not sure that I was ever much more than a stranger to her."

"That's sad," Artie said. Very sad.

"Worse than sad. I failed her. I failed my daughter."

Artie felt a flicker of anger. "Just what were you supposed to do? Quit the Army to move home to be near your ex's family and friends? When she wouldn't even consider doing the same for you?"

One corner of his mouth lifted, but the crooked smile lacked humor. "You know the worst thing we can do in life is run on automatic? Thinking everything is as it should be? Not evaluating? I'm evaluating now, and I'm not liking what I see of myself."

Artie sighed, then rose to freshen their coffee. "Funny how life makes us reevaluate ourselves."

"You, too? Is that what was going on that got you put on leave?"

"You could say that." She nearly slammed the mugs on the table, then remembered that Boyd had bought some kind of apple cinnamon coffee cake. She pulled it out of the fridge, opened it and put in on the table with a knife and two plates. "Remind me not to let you do the shopping again. You buy too many treats."

He shook his head, that lopsided smile remaining. "You deserve it, especially if this crap keeps up."

"Hah! Seriously, Boyd, does the crap ever stop?"

"Guess not." He cut himself a healthy portion and put it on a plate. "Just depends on what kind of crap."

"No kidding."

"And some is worse than others."

He ate half the cake he'd cut for himself and pushed the rest of the cake toward her. "You need some, too."

She took a small slice but stared at it as if it were alien food. It *did* smell good, however. Probably would have been better if she'd heated it.

"So the hike," she pressed, wanting the rest of the story while he was still talking. Before he clammed up.

He just shook his head. "The brain is an amazing thing. Especially when it gets screwed up. Or maybe the gut. God knows which one rules the roost at a given time."

"Don't I know it." Memories of her baton striking Billy Lauer. Purely a gut reaction, just as her continuing reaction to it was in her gut, squirming around like some creature trying to break loose. She could hide it in the recesses of her brain but the rest of her body wasn't letting her forget.

"The hike," he said, taking another piece of cake. "My penance. Working off a fury that seems boundless. Waiting for something to ease the pain, frustrated that I can't get to my daughter. Dealing with a whole load of stuff from my past that there's no way to fix now."

"That sounds like a heck of a lot." More than the things she worried about. A lifetime of regrets? Because that's what it sounded like and she simply couldn't imagine the burden.

He shrugged. "I'll get through it. I always do sooner or later, but this is a big one. A messed-up life."

"You didn't mess *everything* up!"

"Maybe just the really important parts, like marriage and fatherhood." He eyed her. "Was Herman always there for you?"

She looked down, feeling oddly embarrassed, perhaps by her good fortune. But she wouldn't lie. "He is, was, always there for me."

"And *that*," Boyd said, slapping his palm on the table, "is exactly what Linda never had from *me*. I was almost never there. And I sure as hell wasn't there when she was raped two months ago."

"Oh, my God." The words seeped from Artie, barely passing her lips. She screwed her eyes shut, turned her hands into fists and let the pain slice through her. *Rape.*

"Yeah," he said roughly. "Yeah. Brutal. She's only sixteen, for the love of God, and all I want is to be there with her but she doesn't want to see me. Can you blame her? I sure as hell can't!"

He jumped up and she heard the front door slam behind him.

Her eyes remained squeezed closed, her hands fisted until her nails cut into her palms.

No words. No way to comprehend the magnitude of what this man was facing right now.

No wonder he was walking from one end of the continent to the other.

OUTSIDE, JACKETLESS AND not caring, Boyd kicked savagely at snowbanks and got little pleasure from it. He needed a punching bag. Something to hit really hard. Something to be on the receiving end of his fury.

Because it never stopped seething inside him, making him unfit for any but the most casual company. The PTSD had been pretty bad after his discharge, but it had started quieting, thank God.

But not before it had proved to be Shelley's last straw. He sure as hell wasn't the man she'd thought she'd married, and all those years and miles that had separated them because of the Army had fractured it all, he thought. But the bouts of rage he sometimes felt from the PTSD had been the last straw.

He'd never taken them out on Shelley or Linda, had tried to take the episodes away from them, but apparently he'd never gotten far enough away. But it had grown better, a lot better. Until this.

Like a rocket-propelled grenade bearing down on her?

That was the feeling he'd left her with? What the hell had he done? What the hell had he forgotten doing during those episodes of black rage? Or the bouts of heavy drinking?

He'd gotten it under control, but too late. Shelley and his daughter were gone.

Now all he could do was hike until he was too weary for self-loathing to overwhelm him. Until he was too weary to be constantly on edge waiting for Shelley's phone call telling him that Linda wanted to see him at last.

Although he wasn't at all sure that Shelley would keep her promise, not after that last phone call. The only thing he could be certain of was that he hadn't been capable of sitting in North Carolina, working his construction job and just waiting. Waiting endlessly. At least this hike made him feel he was heading toward resolution. Toward being able to hug his daughter again. Or just sit with her and listen to her.

Simple things to wish for, things he'd allowed to slip for too long.

He shoved his hands into his jeans pockets and looked up at the sky. Streetlamps caught gently falling snow, turning the flakes into gold, sometimes scattering the light into tiny prisms.

And once again it was Artie who called him back.

"Damn it, Boyd, get your butt in here. No way am I going to let you freeze to death in my front yard!"

Shaking himself, he headed for the door. Somehow he had to find a resolution with Linda. There had to be a way.

In the meantime he had Artie and her father to concern him. He was in no way ready to dismiss those threats, no matter how weak they seemed on the surface. Not when he'd seen those footprints outside. Not when her father had been indirectly threatened.

Given what was going on right under his nose, indulging his own self-hatred—which when he thought about it, might well be self-pity—he had more important matters on his plate right now.

Such as who might intend Artie and her father harm. And why.

INSIDE, THE CHRISTMAS tree still glowed with blue lights. The fire blazed quietly on the hearth. And the instant Boyd hit the warmth inside, the snowflakes that had sprinkled all over him began to melt. A small thing, especially with the fire so near.

Without asking, Artie brought him a hot mug of cocoa. Dropping cross-legged to the floor, he reached for it, thanking her.

For a little while, other than the crackle of the fire, the house remained sealed in winter silence.

Then Artie spoke. "I'm not quite sure I understand the problem with your daughter. Why didn't you just get on a plane and go? At least then you'd be nearby."

"The thought occurred to me. Believe me." He swigged the hot cocoa, not caring it singed his tongue.

"Then why the hike?"

"Because Shelley, my ex, told me not to come, that Linda wasn't ready to see me, that she was already messed up enough by the rape. Then she told me Linda's shrink said not to come."

"Good God. But if it's like that, why'd she tell you about the rape in the first place?"

He stared off into space, then eventually said in rough voice, "Punishment."

"Cruelty," Artie said sharply. "Stay away but here's the awful thing that happened and we don't want you."

"Yeah. Maybe. Well, I could hardly sit on my hands waiting. Shelley promised to give me a call the minute Linda changed her mind, so I decided to hike off all the feelings that were driving me to no good end. I mean, how would my daughter react if I showed up in Seattle ready to tear the town apart?"

Artie sighed, then slipped off the recliner to sit beside him on the floor. "I see."

"I'm angry, Artie. I want to *do* something for Linda. But what? The cops evidently have the creep, so I'm not needed for finding him. And I'm sure not needed within a block or two like a simmering volcano. No amount of anger I feel is going to fix this, so I need to manage it. Walking is good for that."

"Not gonna tear the creep's face off, huh?"

Boyd felt an unexpected lightening in his chest. An almost-smile reached his face. "Or break his neck. Unfortunately."

"Ah, that's too tame," she replied.

"Nah." He returned his attention to the fire. "What Linda needs from me, if she ever wants any of me again, is kindness and understanding, not fury. Anger seems to have become my general reaction to life."

"I hear that's not uncommon in vets."

His answer took time in coming. "That may be true. There's a lot that has to be bottled up."

"Anger is at least safe."

He turned his head to look straight at her. "Safe for who?"

A GOOD QUESTION, Artie thought. Safe for him, maybe? Not to let in pain if you could hold it away with anger? But safe for others? Probably not.

She also knew she was getting into deep waters here. She didn't have the experience or training to get into anyone's psychology and certainly not Boyd's. Time to back out before she risked appearing judgmental. Hell, she had no business judging anyone else, not after Lauer. Not after what she'd done.

She put her mug aside and leaned back on her elbows, her legs still crossed. "We make a pair," was all she said.

At last a small chuckle escaped him. "Here we sit next to a Christmas tree and I doubt either of us could be any bluer than those lights."

"A pity party?" she asked dryly.

"We seem to be edging into one. In my own case I think I'm spending too much time kicking myself for what I've done. I did it. Time to move and find some way to fix what I can."

"Sometimes easier to say than to do."

"Can't disagree. But when it comes to Linda I got to thinking this afternoon, after talking to Shelley, that I've still got parental rights. For some reason she didn't try to get sole custody."

He paused, then shrugged. "Maybe she didn't think I'd be around enough to become a problem, so why duke it out? And she was evidently right. Until now."

"What will you do about it?"

"That remains to be seen. First I get myself into a

more reasonable frame of mind. Linda doesn't need a wreck for a father."

Then he leaned back on one elbow, stretching his legs out, turning toward her. "And what about you, Artie? You're not saying a damn thing about what happened to you just before we met. Not one thing about why someone would want to scare you. Not a thing about how this could involve your father."

But this wasn't the time for naked truths, she thought. Not her own anyway. She wasn't ready to give voice to the turmoil inside her.

But she was ready for something else. Firelight played over Boyd's strong face. Blue light from the tree illuminated the shadows, emphasizing the determination she saw in him.

In that instant, she felt the electric shock of overpowering hunger. It zinged through her, both unexpected and unwanted. Not now. Not this stranger with a huge pile of problems that made her own seem trivial by comparison.

Not a man who'd be leaving in a few days, homing in on his daughter, more focused on helping Linda than anything else in his life.

Not a fling. She'd never been the type to want a fling, a good thing in this small town. Then she wondered why she cared. What was wrong with a romp in the hay, just this once?

Boyd's eyes had narrowed. Had his face come closer to hers? She hoped so, and realized her breathing had changed, as if the air were being sucked out and she couldn't inhale deeply enough.

Excitement found every nerve ending in her body. She had to force herself to remain still, not to reach for the wonder lying just beside her.

Then he spoke the question that cracked every wall she'd tried to place between them.

"Artie?"

She reached for him.

BOYD WAS ASTONISHED that she wanted him, but even more astonished that despite his self-imposed punishment and anger, he could feel this sudden surge of desire.

In a split second, Artie tugged him out of the real world into a place of hunger and light. Everything else on the planet vanished as he pulled her close, feeling every inch of her slender body pressed to the length of his.

He spared one last hope that neither of them would regret this, but then he didn't care at all.

He just wanted Artie with every fiber of his being. Just Artie. No one else. No other woman. It was all blindingly new, somehow. All of it. All of her.

When she tugged at his sweatshirt, he pulled it away, hungering for the touch of her hands on his naked skin. Her touch everywhere and all over.

He shed his clothes quickly. Hers proved a little more difficult with those damn buttoned jeans, but she gave a little giggle and helped him get rid of them.

Then they lay there on the rug, two gleaming bodies, bare for every touch of eyes and hands.

"God, you're beautiful," he whispered as he began

to stroke every inch of her he could reach. Her skin, smooth as satin, warm beneath his palms and fingers. Her curves delicious perfection. Her breasts small and firm with large nipples. They hardened, calling for his mouth.

But he touched them with his hands first, cradling her breast and brushing his thumb across her nipple.

Her breath grew ragged. Her body began a gentle squirming that only aroused him more. As if that was even possible.

A breathless, tiny laugh escaped her as she rolled even more closely to him. "My turn, gorgeous."

He was happy to comply, rolling a bit more to his back, giving her free rein to enjoy him as she chose.

And man, did she choose. He closed his eyes, giving himself up to her spell, feeling her hands search out every bit of him from his own tiny nipples to his swollen groin. The shocks of pleasure ran through him until he felt every nerve of his body burning for her.

"Artie..." His voice had grown thick.

"Yeah, yeah," she said, panting a bit but sounding a little humorous, as well. "Wait a little longer, big guy."

But he didn't need to wait that much longer. Rising up, she straddled him, wide open to his touch. Reaching down, he felt the nub of her desire swollen for his touch.

"God, that's so good it almost hurts," she whispered brokenly. "Boyd..."

No words necessary now. Finding himself, he slid into her moist, hot depths. In an instant the blaze welded them together. She rocked on him and he reached up to cradle her breasts, teasing her more.

They rode in the waves of an eternal sea that carried them from crest to crest, each higher and stronger than the one before.

Then the sea became a tsunami, sweeping them away into a place beyond the mind. Beyond earth.

To a gentler shore.

To a peace neither of them had known in a long while.

RESTING BENEATH A blanket that Boyd had rustled up from the back of the couch, they held each other tightly, limbs feeling weak but oddly strong at the same time.

Boyd caressed her hair, dropping gentle kisses on her shoulder. The scent of their lovemaking perfumed the air around them. Artie sighed quietly, moving her fingers over his smooth skin. She felt one scar, a long one, near the base of his spine, but said nothing. He'd gone to war after all, and she didn't want to remind him. Not now in these minutes out of time, minutes the rest of the world still hadn't intruded on.

"I'm luxuriating," she murmured eventually.

"Me, too. I could stay here forever."

Except forever wasn't going to happen. At last a cold trickle of reality reached beneath the blanket. She wanted to bury it, but it wouldn't go away. Especially when she thought of Herman. Her dad. Now threatened, too. But why?

At last she gave in, sitting up even though moving away from Boyd felt as if she were tearing her own skin off.

"God."

"I know." He sat up, too. "I know."

"Cocoa," she said after the sense of loss eased. She reached for her clothes and pulled them on. He wasn't far behind. But at the last minute he pulled her close and kissed her deeply. "Another time?"

How could she refuse? She wanted time after time with him. "Yes."

Then he smiled, helped her up and walked to the kitchen with her. "Does Herman sleep through the night?"

"Mostly. He gets up earlier than he used to, but sometimes he gets a nap in the afternoon. Things change as we get older, I guess. Clara says that she used to have to be dragged out of bed in the mornings, but now she's up before the birds. You?"

He shook his head briefly. "I have nothing resembling a sleep schedule. I take what I can get when I can get it."

The war, she suspected. And maybe now, too.

Once again they faced each other across the table.

"I'm so sorry about your daughter," she said into a silence that seemed to be growing heavier, the joys of their lovemaking easing away into memory.

"Me, too." He sipped the hot cocoa. "I haven't often felt helpless in my life, but I do now."

She wrapped her hands around her mug, wanting the warmth in her chilling fingers. "You said you might be able to do something? Custody?"

"Yeah." He stared into space. "I still can't imagine why she didn't try to deny me any custody at all, but she didn't. So that must give me legal rights."

"I'd think so." Once again she ached for this man. "I wish there was something I could do to help."

"Nobody can," he answered roughly. "I made this mess. Maybe what I need is a lawyer."

"So you can see your daughter?"

"So I can find out her mental and physical state. God knows I'm not going to force myself on her. But that call with Shelley made me wonder just how much of this problem *she* is. Anyway, I've got to know more about Linda than Shelley's reports."

That revealed a lot. Artie drew a long breath. "You don't trust her."

"Maybe I never should have. Or maybe I should have figured it out sooner."

"I suppose love pretty much blinds us." Not ever having been truly in love, she could only imagine it.

"And maybe we should wait long enough to figure it out. A cooling-off period."

Artie grinned in spite of everything. "How likely is that?"

Boyd returned her smile. "Not very."

"Probably one of the reasons most marriages end in the first year. Eyes open up."

"That's a depressing thought. Think of all the hopes and dreams, how high falling in love makes us feel."

Which was exactly a situation Artie needed to keep in mind right now. Their lovemaking had made her high as a kite. But that couldn't be all of it, shouldn't be if a future were involved. But there was no future here, she reminded herself. Blinders could do little harm.

They were on their second cup of cocoa when Boyd broached the difficult subject. "You changed your mind about those threats."

"When they mentioned Herman, yeah. Why are they telling me to think of him? Not just about myself." Artie looked down, trying to deal with that. "I can't imagine any possible reason."

"Except to scare you," he pointed out. "They must feel they haven't done a very good job of it so far."

"Or maybe it's just one guy. I don't know. I can't tell from the voice on the phone." She looked at him. "Boyd, I don't scare easily, but that last call started to frighten me."

Then there were the footprints behind her house. She didn't want to think about those, either, but she did. "Those prints you found in the snow out back? Who the hell would be out in this weather? And just to scope my house."

"Maybe they thought they wouldn't be detected."

"Well, they sure as hell could have broken in right then. You were out doing all that shoveling."

"That's a point. But maybe the guy isn't brave enough to take you one-on-one."

She thought of her baton and what it had done to Billy Lauer. Maybe that was enough to scare a single attacker. She still couldn't believe she hadn't put Lauer in the hospital, though, as hard as she had hit him. But that was the point of the baton, wasn't it? Nonlethal force.

"So what exactly happened that night you picked me up, Artie? Something sure as hell messed with you."

Her gorge rose; the memory became more vivid. Much as she wanted to escape it, she couldn't. It hit her like a shock wave all over again. She choked out the words. "I nearly beat a man to death with my baton. And I'll never forget the way that felt. I'll never trust myself the same way again because I let rage control me."

Then, unable to hold it in any longer, she jumped up and reached the kitchen sink just before she began to vomit. Just as she had right after the incident. As if she could puke out all the violence she had discovered in herself.

Boyd swiftly came to her side, dampening a towel and pressing it to her forehead. "Let it out, let it all out."

Her retching stopped soon, turning into dry heaves that made her sides and stomach ache. At last she leaned weakly against the counter, at once ashamed of herself, yet still grateful that Boyd was there, helping as much as he could.

"Rinse your mouth," he said when she straightened. "Don't swallow."

She obeyed, then turned, feeling the swelling in her eyes, the continued burning in her stomach. "I'm sorry."

"For what? You think I haven't puked my guts out? Sometimes that's the only answer."

She couldn't have asked for a better man at this time. One who understood. Who made no apologies for her. Gratitude washed through her, along with the first inklings of true friendship.

"Thanks." She made her way back to the table and pushed aside the cup of cocoa that looked revolting now. "God, I guess I'm not dealing at all. I thought I was."

"You've been distracted by other things," he pointed out. "Threats. Your father. But everything gets its due. That's one thing I sure as hell have figured out. We get haunted sometimes. Haunted permanently about some things. When you're ready, talk to me. You don't need to hold it in like a time bomb."

And that was precisely what she seemed to be doing. Holding it in, trying not to face it, trying to avoid her horror. That seemed to be doing no good at all.

Her stomach turned over again. "I don't know if I can."

"You'll have to, sooner or later." Now he reached out and took her hand. "When you're ready. But I'm absolutely positive you can't tell me anything I haven't already done or seen."

She closed her eyes, grateful for his touch, accepting slowly that he was probably right. Her one experience couldn't possibly equal what he'd seen at war. But facing it in herself was a different thing.

"I don't know where to begin," she said eventually, her voice ragged.

"Anywhere will do," he said gently. "These things

rarely follow a timeline. Experiences are different from a calendar."

She swallowed, seeking courage. Never before had courage deserted her, but it had right now. For this. "It should be like writing a report."

"If that's what feels more comfortable to you."

She drew another deep breath and blew it out between her lips. He'd shared some terribly important stuff about himself, things that caused him enough anguish to walk across an entire continent in order to deal with them.

"It was a domestic violence call," she said presently. "Get them too often. The Lauers…you could say they're familiar to us. Frequent fliers, we sometimes call them. Bea, the wife, would never press charges and we never saw anything ourselves so we couldn't pursue it."

He nodded. "The victims are terrified, aren't they?"

"That's the least of it."

"But this was different?"

"Oh, God, Boyd, I've never seen it that bad. I was the first to arrive on the scene. Bea was lying in a pool of blood and Billy Lauer was choking her to death. Her eyes were bulging. She couldn't make a sound."

"God!"

"So I pulled my gun and ordered him to stop, to get off her or I'd shoot."

She squeezed her eyes tightly, the images painted in stark detail in her mind. Those images would never leave her. "He didn't listen," she said thickly.

Boyd didn't press her. He let her take whatever time she needed.

"I couldn't shoot," she said, her voice ragged. "They were too close. There were people in apartments around them. I couldn't risk hurting any of them if a bullet went through the walls."

"Smart."

"Smart?" She nearly shouted the word and jumped up from the table. "There was nothing smart about any of it. I should have found a better way."

"What way?"

She sagged against the counter. "I don't know. I keep thinking there *had* to be a better way. Any kind of way."

"But you couldn't find one?"

"I'm not sure I was even thinking at that point. I was seeing red. Scared he'd kill Bea, scared I wouldn't stop him in time and all I wanted was to *kill* that man. Kill. I was murderous."

Again he remained silent, letting her find her way through this morass. As if she ever might.

"I've never wanted to kill anyone before," she said, huge silent tears beginning to roll down her face. "I did the only thing I thought of. Maybe because I was past thinking. I opened my baton and started beating him as hard as I could. I'll never forget the feeling of my baton hitting him. God, it was awful. Just awful!"

"I know."

He probably did. Little consolation in that.

"And then?" he asked, evidently sensing there was more.

Her voice grew even heavier, harsher, approaching sobs. "I got his attention. He came at me. Was reaching for my pistol, punching me again and again. I managed to lock the pistol and throw it behind me, out the front door. Not that it mattered then. Blow after blow."

"He was well past any kind of rationality," Boyd said. He'd risen and was coming closer to her, but not enough to make her feel trapped.

"Then backup arrived." She half covered her mouth, trying to hold all the broken pieces inside herself together somehow. "Almost too late. Outside I just kept throwing up. I couldn't stop. Weakness. Everyone saw it."

"Damn it, Artie, I don't think a single soul saw you as weak at that point."

"I did." The words hung in the air, an ugly miasma of guilt, of fear, of self-doubt.

Boyd drew a step closer, holding his arms out in invitation, but before she could move, she heard her dad's voice.

"My God, Artie, what have they done to you?"

"DAD...GO TO BED."

But Herman was having none of it. "You get out there and sit in front of the fire. Boyd, you make sure it's ablaze. I'll make us all some cocoa."

"Dad..."

"I heard, Artie. I heard most of it. And if you think I'm going back to my damn bed when you've been going through hell, you're mistaken."

Boyd guided Artie to the couch, not to the recliner. He fed more logs into the fire, letting them catch into a brighter fire.

Then he tucked the blanket around Artie and sat close beside her. He'd seen this before, knew there was never going to be any easy solution, but very glad Herman had stepped in. Artie had been too much alone with all this. Way too much.

There was a point, as he knew from personal experience, when you needed some buddies to rely on. Buddies who understood. Boyd understood from the war. Herman understood because this was his daughter.

Damn her self-reliance. It had kept her isolated when she least needed it.

Herman served up the cocoa along with some of the coffee cake. A capable man who'd probably been doing such things all his life. A man who maybe resented having to rely so much on Artie. Like father like daughter, Boyd thought. They were a pair, all right. Inevitably he wondered if Linda was at all like him, and he felt a strong hope that she wasn't. He wouldn't wish anyone to be like him. Not anyone.

Boyd took the bull by the horns, addressing Herman even if Artie didn't want him to. "So, Herman, just how much do you know?"

"Since the blizzard? Since you came walking through my front door? Since I took one look at Artie's face and knew all the way to my soul that something bad had happened to her? And that it wasn't you."

Artie's head jerked a little. "Dad..."

"Quit trying to hush me, Artemis. Just because I lose my memory sometimes, forget where I am, doesn't mean I got stupid. You hear me?"

Artie nodded slowly, looking forlorn, still too pale.

"I don't sleep too well anymore," Herman said. "Littlest sounds can wake me. Not like my younger days when I could have slept through the house burning down. But now…now I wake up. You two think I don't know what was going on in front of the fire out here?"

Artie gasped. "Dad!"

Herman shrugged. "Normal. Expect it from you from time to time. There hasn't been enough of it around here. Always thought you needed a good boyfriend, or a good girlfriend. Never had either. I was beginning to worry that maybe I was part of the cause of that."

Artie shook her head. Boyd watched feeling a mild amusement. His affection for Artie and her father was growing.

Herman hadn't lost himself, though, or slipped his place in time. Right then his memory was as sharp as a tack. "I heard what you were telling Boyd. Why the hell didn't you tell me? Damn it, child, if anyone in this world can be trusted with your feelings, don't you think it's me?"

Artie's voice croaked, almost like laryngitis. "I couldn't trust myself with them."

Herman nodded. "Drink some of that cocoa. 'Bout time you started being human like the rest of us. We all got feelings we can't trust unless we talk to ourselves or somebody else. Ask Boyd, here."

"It's true," he agreed. Although he was guilty of a lot of failure to share himself. Mile after mile of it. Maybe years of it. That didn't make Herman wrong.

"So you saved a woman's life by beating that bastard nearly to death and you're blaming yourself. What for?"

Boyd answered for her, despite realizing she might resent it. *Someone* had to talk about this. "She thinks she lost her self-control. That she should have found a better way. That she let anger rule her."

Artie found enough energy to glare at him. "I can talk for myself."

Boyd sighed.

"Not doing enough of it," was Herman's judgment. "You're turning into a bottle that's about to blow like a Molotov cocktail. Where the hell did you get that from?"

"You," she answered, for the first time showing a genuine spark.

"And you think I never talked to your mother? Guess you weren't listening. Well, you were just a kid. Anyway, at least you talked to Boyd here, and I'm glad I heard."

Artie at last sipped some cocoa. It went down easily this time, but she felt some resentment that her father was trying to tell her how to live, but hadn't he always? Didn't mean she had to listen. She'd been making her own decisions for a long time now.

Herman waved a hand. "You won't listen to me," he said, as if reading her mind. Maybe he could. "Never did. But what's with these phone calls? I knew something was bothering you, but you never said a damn word."

"There wasn't much to say about it," she answered,

mostly truthfully. Glad to escape any further discussion about the Lauer incident. She'd already said enough about that, exposed herself quite enough, at least for now.

"Nothing much," she repeated.

Herman harrumphed, a sound that always indicated that he didn't believe her.

"Okay," she said presently. "I've had a handful of calls. One of them told me to watch my back. Another mentioned you, as if you're at risk. That's the one that really set me off, if you want the truth."

Herman nodded. "Anything else I need to know?"

Boyd answered since she seemed reluctant. "A couple of the calls came over your landline."

At that, Herman slammed his recliner into the upright position. "Nobody knows that number except your department!"

Artie shook her head. "It must have slipped out somehow."

"And that's why Gage was here tonight, wasn't it? He's aware. What the hell are they doing about it?"

"Trying to track the calls. Find out who made them."

Herman nodded. "Seems like little enough."

Artie spread her hands. "What else can they do, Dad? They're already overstretched as it is, and since the storm they must be buried in more important things. I can handle this. I always have."

"Nothing like this," Herman grumped. Then he eyed Boyd. "You planning to stay for a while?"

Boyd nodded reluctantly. He didn't want to make

Artie feel any worse. "Just a little backup. Artie probably won't need me at all."

At that, Herman laughed. "No, she'll never admit she might. Even if it comes out that she does."

"Oh, Dad, for Pete's sake! Quit talking about me like I'm not here. You don't know what…"

Her father interrupted her, "Artemis, I been raising you for damn near thirty years and I know you like the back of my hand. I just don't usually remind you of that. All your life you never wanted any help. I *know* you can take care of yourself. You almost always have. But this could be different. Especially with you being all upset about that Lauer and what you had to do."

Artie gave up the struggle. Her dad was turning into a battering ram, not that she hadn't seen that before, and he was in a mood to take charge of her and her decisions. Well, let him. Might as well make him feel better, even if she knew in the end this would all come down to how she handled herself.

Herman settled back on his recliner, rocking it gently as he stared into the fire and sipped cocoa. The fire blazed cheerfully, probably the most cheerful thing in this house right now. The Christmas tree paled by comparison.

Boyd stirred, putting his arm around her shoulders. That felt so right and good that it was all she could do not to turn into him. But not with her father right there.

Boyd, she found herself thinking, might be the best thing to come out of all this.

A while later, Herman spoke again. "You think it's this Lauer guy threatening you?"

"Not likely." She felt Boyd's arm tighten around her a bit, supportive. God, was she actually accepting a man's support? But she didn't pull away from it. Felt no desire to.

"Why not?" Herman asked.

"Because he's still in a cell. He can't make any phone calls from there. He probably won't even be offered bail until his arraignment. Maybe tomorrow if things get rolling again. So it can't be him."

"Hmm," Herman said, sounding doubtful.

Boyd spoke. "The man have any friends? And why would they be after you anyway? The incident happened. The evidence is there."

Artie shook her head. "Doesn't work that way. If Bea won't press charges, then there has to be a witness who can prove Lauer did all that damage to her himself. I'm the only one who saw it all. So…I'd have to testify at a trial."

Boyd swore quietly. "That could be what this is all about. His friends might be doing this."

"Like they can stop me. If this goes to trial, I'll get subpoenaed as a witness. Even if I quit my job, I can't get out of that."

As she spoke, she felt her stomach sink. *Forget about it*, the voice on the phone had said. *Forget about it*.

Forget what she'd seen? Develop a hole in her memory under oath, or before a trial?

For the second time that night she felt sick to her stomach.

"That leaves only one option," Boyd said.

Artie couldn't disagree. And now her father was a pawn on this creep's chessboard.

A threat against her dad scared Artie more than a threat against herself.

Herman spoke. "Seems like it might be good to have Boyd stay awhile, Artie. I'm not in the shape I used to be. Although I could probably still do a good job with a tire iron."

The way she had with her baton. God, could it get any worse?

Chapter Twelve

When morning arrived, Artie awoke to find herself leaning into Boyd, wrapped securely in his arms. She felt as if she could stay there forever.

The fire was dying to small flames and embers. From the kitchen came enticing aromas.

Herman must be cooking. The usual concern tried to edge its way into her mind. If he forgot what he was doing…

But she smelled no burning, and maybe she was over-worrying the situation all the time. Her dad still had his good spells. Quite a few of them. And when they came, they lasted awhile.

He was not completely lost in his disease. Far from it. Fear of the future consumed her even more than the present worries, and maybe it was high time that she took the good spells as a gift.

Boyd stirred. "I hope you slept as well as I did," he said, his voice rusty.

She had, better than she'd slept in a while. Much as she hated doing it, she straightened, leaving his embrace behind. *Don't get attached*, she warned herself.

Not now. He was leaving as soon as he could, resuming his private march into a hell he was still plumbing, a hell he didn't yet know the depths of.

She allowed the blanket to fall away and stretched. God, she needed a shower. If Boyd did, she couldn't tell. His scents were as enticing as any emerging from the kitchen.

"I need to look in on Herman."

"Okay. If it's all right, I'll take a quick shower and throw my things into the wash. Unless you want to go first."

"You first." She really *did* need to look in on her father. Last night was fresh in her mind, reminding her of the man who had raised her since birth, the man she would love for the rest of her days, whether he was gone or not.

She hoped that man was still with her this morning.

Bright morning light was beginning to pour through the kitchen window. The storm was over.

Herman hummed quietly as he cooked bacon. Rye bread was toasting. Coffee already made.

"Smells wonderful," Artie said.

Herman turned from the stove with a smile. "It should. I swear there's nothing better to start a day than bacon. You want scrambled eggs?"

"Boyd just headed for the shower."

Herman frowned faintly. "The bacon'll keep but I wish I hadn't started the toast."

"He said he'd be quick. I don't think he'd want to interrupt you."

"Probably not. Seems like a thoughtful young man."

He did, she thought, extremely thoughtful considering the baggage he carried. Sitting at the table, she accepted a mug of the fresh coffee.

"So," her father said, returning to the bacon, "did anything I said last night penetrate that stubborn wall of yours?"

"Maybe."

Herman chuckled. "Not likely you'd admit it. But I'd pay attention to these calls if I were you. Somebody's got a burr under his saddle and doesn't seem like he wants to forget about it. Maybe not that Lauer guy, but like I said, he's got friends. Must have. Somebody who might have a big grudge against you."

Artie couldn't deny it, but she shook her head anyway. She was still feeling raw from her revelations last night, from the things she'd admitted to. From her own pain and self-doubt that weren't going away just because someone said they weren't unusual or were even justified. She had to deal with her *feelings*. And they weren't likely to yield to reason.

"Let's talk about something else," she suggested.

"Sure. Then we can all *think* about it while the world gets on the move again. While you become reachable."

"Damn it, Dad!"

"Gotta look it in the eye, and it's not like you to ignore it."

He turned off the burner and lifted the last strips of bacon onto a plate covered with a paper towel. "I'm more worried about you than me," he said flatly. "You don't need to tell me there's only one way you can be prevented from testifying against that monster."

"That might not be what this is all about." But she knew it was. In her heart of hearts, she knew it all revolved around Lauer.

The timing practically shouted it. But with Lauer in a cell, just how far were his friends prepared to go? They might wind up in cells, too, with charges just as bad.

But what else could they hope to achieve? She was the only eyewitness. Her backup had arrived only as she had overpowered Lauer with her baton. No one else had seen that Lauer was the one who was strangling his wife. Lauer could plead that someone had broken into his apartment. Could even claim Artie herself had beaten Bea like she'd beaten him. Not that that would stand up in court, not against a cop sworn to tell the truth.

Without Artie's testimony, there'd be no trial and the prosecutor might have to deal for a lighter sentence for Billy Lauer.

God Almighty. She didn't even want to *think* about what had happened but now she might have to replay it all again. In a courtroom. In front of others who would see her rage, her loss of control. Some who might even feel some sympathy for Lauer's treatment at her hands.

While juries tended to support cops, they didn't always. A lot depended on their overall reaction to the case. A decent defense attorney might even make it sound as if Lauer had suffered the worst harm.

Damn, she should have gone with the ambulance that night. Should have let her bruises be documented in photos and a doctor's report. To substantiate her own claims about what had happened.

She put her head in her hands, trying not to think about the several ways in which she seemed to have lost her mind that night. Something in her had snapped. How could she be sure it wouldn't happen again? How could she be sure she could trust herself to run around this county with a weapon on her hip?

As if out of nowhere, a plate full of eggs, bacon and toast appeared in front of her. For the first time she realized that Boyd was there, too, sitting at the side of the table.

"Man," he said. "Herman, this looks like heaven."

Herman laughed. "I'm not helpless in the kitchen despite what Artie thinks."

She lifted her head and looked at him. She felt not a muscle in her face move. Frozen.

"Of course, maybe she's right," Herman said as he poured fresh coffee, then joined them. "Sometimes I'm not as well put together as I used to be. Can't guarantee I won't forget I'm cooking and start a fire."

He waved his hand around the kitchen. "See all she's done for me to make this place safer? All that induction stuff. That toaster oven. And didn't I just use the gas stove?"

At that, feeling frozen or not, Artie tipped up one corner of her mouth. "Guess I need to replace that, too."

"Kinda expensive." Herman paused, a slice of

bacon between his fingers. "Okay, okay. I get it. Don't have to like it, but I get it. Doesn't mean I can't still start a fire."

Artie just shook her head. "Gas is dangerous, Dad. And that stove is so old, what if the pilot light goes out? Won't matter if you're cooking at all."

Herman grumbled. "Look, can we eat without getting one of us upset?"

Artie nodded. This was a pointless argument anyway. That induction stove would come whether he wanted it. But her dad was right. She didn't want to consider all the reasons over breakfast.

Boyd spoke, carrying them past the awkward moment. "This is a great breakfast, Herman. You can cook for me at any time."

Herman laughed, a sound that was wheezier now than in his youth, but not by that much. "You're on. But the menu is limited. Artie's mom was the kitchen boss, wasn't she, Artie?"

"Definitely."

"She tried to teach you once in a while," her dad recalled. "Not that you were having any part of it."

Artie shrugged a shoulder. "I hated it. I still hate it, but I couldn't tell you why."

"Just wasn't your thing. We all have stuff like that. All your mom said about it was that one day you were going to learn whether you liked it or not."

"She didn't quite succeed," Artie answered dryly.

"Frozen meals," Herman nodded. "They're good enough."

Of course they weren't, but Artie felt she had quite

enough guilt just now and wasn't about to add any over nutrition.

Boyd spoke. "Plenty of times I'd have given my eyeteeth for a frozen meal. Dried food just isn't quite the same."

In an instant, Afghanistan and the Army marched into the room with them.

God. Artie nearly pushed her plate aside, then decided she didn't want to hurt her dad's feelings. She bit into another strip of crunchy bacon, tasting only sawdust.

Herman answered him, "Bet you ate a lot of that. Army, you said?"

"Yeah. Freeze-dried foods are lighter, easier to carry more of it. Of course, when you got back to base, there was plenty of fast food available."

Surprised, Artie looked at him. "Fast food?"

"A few of the chains had outlets there. Like the food court at a mall."

"Wow. I never thought of that."

"It's one way to get young people to eat enough. Besides, it wasn't long before you started craving a taste of home. A burger and fries topped the list. Pizza was pretty popular, too."

"For the most part, the closest we get to fast food around here is Maude's diner or the truck stop. Or that pizza place just outside town."

"Maybe that Mexican restaurant will finally open," Herman said.

Artie spoke. "I'm not holding my breath. They've

been trying for quite a while. I never asked why they were having so much trouble."

"Money," Herman answered bluntly. "It'd be nice if this town ever came out of the doldrums again."

BOYD, PAYING ATTENTION to every detail, noted that the pinched look around Artie's eyes had eased somewhat. At least she'd achieved a few minutes of distraction with the conversation revolving around food.

But he knew damn well the other thoughts would return. He knew damn well how they did, how they simply wouldn't go away until you learned to live with them. That took time.

The Lauer incident and now this fear for her father. There hadn't been a call since yesterday but that didn't mean a thing. Carrying dishes to the sink, he stared out at the brilliant winter day and felt it coming.

The threat was real. No matter how much Artie might try to dismiss it. It was real and now that the weather had cleared, there'd be nothing to get in the way.

The back of his neck prickled as it hadn't since Afghanistan. He could feel it coming.

"ALL RIGHT, GENIUS," Willie said to Joe, "you got a brilliant idea? Once the plows gets here and we gets out easy, what then? Walk up to her door with that there sawed-off and shoot? Like you ain't in enough trouble already."

"We already got to that damn house," Joe said.

Willie couldn't rightly argue that. "Damn near killed ourselves on them roads."

"We still got there."

"And I saw another SOB there. She ain't alone."

"The guy was skinny. Shoveled snow like he got orders. Wimp."

"Skinny, huh?" Willie rolled that around in his brain, his thinking fueled by a longneck. "We ain't skinny."

No chance of that, Willie thought proudly, patting the years of beer on his belly with pride. Some of them football players had bellies even bigger. Thinking about how they crashed through other players made him smile as he swigged more beer.

Yeah, him and Joe had the edge in that department.

As THE DAY brightened and the brilliant sunlight began to crust the snow, Boyd announced he was going to finish the shoveling out front, including Clara's house.

Artie immediately said she'd help. "I'm going stir-crazy."

"I hear you." But for once, Boyd wasn't in the mood to play the polite guest. "But you're going to keep your butt inside and keep an eye on things. Like Herman."

Artie returned a rebellious look but didn't argue. The way Boyd's mind was made up, he figured a fight with Artie right now might turn into a nuclear explosion. He'd seen the spark and fire in that woman. He felt a surprising amount of relief when she gave him a mulish look but didn't disagree. Hell, she even planted her bottom in the recliner near Herman's.

And Herman had gone back to watching some seasonal cartoon or other. Boyd hoped that wasn't a bad sign. And there stood the Christmas tree, always on, with not one cheery thing about it at the moment.

Ah, hell. Boyd left by the back door through the mudroom. Booted up, wearing his parka, he was ready enough for the cold day.

He paused on the back step, though, and scanned for the footprints he'd seen. Nothing toward the alley. Snow must have filled them in. But right behind the house, where heat escaped, the prints remained in the crust.

Boyd went to get the shovel, but the first thing he did was cover up those remaining prints. If the creep decided to take another peek, he'd leave fresh tracks behind.

The sun began at last to crust the snow. It also felt warm on the shoulders of Boyd's parka and began heating the inside. He pulled the zipper down partway and resumed shoveling Clara's walk.

He was doing more than moving snow, however. He was keeping an eye on the activity on the street, looking for anything untoward.

Hard to tell on a street that had become busy with other shovelers like himself. He joined in the long-distance camaraderie, at least by waving to others. No one seemed inclined in these temperatures to gather for a confab. Which was good because he didn't need any distractions. Not now.

Since he could think of only one way the caller could prevent Artie from testifying in a trial, he

couldn't afford any distraction, not one. He'd protect
Artie and Herman with his life, if necessary. Part of
that meant remaining on alert.

But night. When night came the danger would be
higher than it was on this bright street. At night he
would have to be on highest alert.

Because he absolutely did not believe this was
going to end with a few phone calls.

ARTIE FUMED AT being stuck inside, even though she
understood Boyd's reasoning. She was also getting
sick of the sound of cartoons. Her dad had been so
good this morning. Was he backsliding now?

She kept shooting looks his way, wondering if there
was any way to tell. At least he'd dressed himself this
morning. Some days he never got out of his robe.

She went to make more coffee even though she
didn't want any. Boyd might like it when he came in
from the cold.

God, being stuck in the house like this was going
to drive her absolutely over the edge. She needed to
work. She needed to be out in the world, associating
with other people, helping them as she could, protecting when necessary. Her job fulfilled her even on the
days when it was boring.

Now this. Yeah, even on temporary suspension she
could have gone out, walked around, talked to people, hit the grocery, picked up something at Maude's.
Anything except being stuck in this house because
of threats, trying not to pace because it might disturb

her father, especially if he really was that absorbed in the cartoon.

Which she honestly hoped he wasn't. Stifling a sigh, she *did* pace a little, quietly, away from the TV. God, she needed to *do* something.

Midafternoon, she got a welcome surprise. Boyd opened the door and leaned in. "Look who came to visit. I'm taking the shovel round back."

Then Clara stepped into the house, her cheeks rosy and a huge smile on her face. She wore her calf-length, hooded red wool coat with faux white fur surrounding her face. Maybe not the warmest clothing for this climate, but perfect nonetheless.

She greeted Artie with a hug as Boyd disappeared back out the front door. "You're looking about as well as I'd expect from anyone with cabin fever."

Artie smiled. "How'd you guess?"

"I think I have a case, too." As Clara started unbuttoning her coat, she called out, "Hey, Herman! Am I less interesting that that damn TV?"

Herman turned immediately, first looking surprised, then grinning ear to ear. "Clara!" He rose instantly and opened his arms to her.

Clara shrugged out of her coat, letting Artie take it, then walked into Herman's embrace. "Been missing you, old man. Dang storm froze every bit of life, didn't it? Oh, the Christmas tree is beautiful. Letitia would have loved it."

Artie held her breath, fearing the past tense in her father's reply. Relief filled her as he stayed firmly in the present.

"She would have. Artie and Boyd put it up for me. I like remembering, Clara."

She stepped back, her hands on his upper arms, and nodded. "I like remembering, too."

"You look beautiful today."

"It's all the color the cold put in my cheeks. Don't go overboard there."

But Clara did look great, Artie thought, feeling drab in her jeans and a blue fleece pullover. Clara had managed to put together a green wool suit, dressed to the nines as it were. But then Clara had always had a sense of style even here where jeans were the uniform of the day.

"Now," said Clara, "are you going to turn off that TV so I can whip you at dominoes?"

"Whip me? You wish."

Ten minutes later Artie had set up the folding table and chairs, and brought them both coffee.

Then she wondered where Boyd had gone.

BOYD HAD CHECKED out Artie's backyard again, hunting for even the least indication that someone had been there.

Nothing. He wasn't sure whether that was good or bad. A stalker might keep away for a few days, he supposed. Planning. Or not wanting to leave an obvious trail. He couldn't dismiss those footprints he'd seen, though. Bad weather, too bad for an ordinary stroll. Too close to the house, as if someone wanted to peek through windows.

Whoever it had been was up to no good.

That tightening through his neck and shoulders returned. Gearing up for action, for something bad that lay around the corner. For an unseen threat.

He'd lived a long time with those sensations and he'd learned never to ignore them.

He scanned the houses around that might give anyone a good view of Artie's place, but saw nothing to concern him in the windows.

Then he headed next door to Clara's, her key in his pocket, his eyes scanning constantly. She wanted him to get the large casserole she'd made for dinner and bring it over. Easy enough.

Better yet, he could check another area for anything suspicious.

This threat didn't have to be coming from far away, though. It might be arising from just down this street or a block away. It could come fast.

He started thinking about what he could use as a weapon in Artie's house, because he was damned if he was going to use her baton or service pistol. She needed those. He was trained to use a whole lot of other stuff. Darn near anything, come to that.

Clara's house showed no sign of any unwanted visitors. The last sign had been those footprints he'd seen marching toward the back of Artie's house and they'd been nearly covered at the time.

None to be seen, not even the remains of the first ones. With the snow developing a crust, an intruder would have a harder time concealing his passage.

One good thing to think about. Right now the only one.

Then the wind whipped up and blew snow in his face. So okay, it wasn't all crusted yet. Didn't seem to be getting packed much, either. Footprints might still vanish in minutes.

Damn it all to hell!

THE CASSEROLE WAS warmly received. Artie appeared delighted. "I can't thank you enough, Clara!"

"I know how you love to cook," Clara answered wryly. "Anyway, it's nothing special. Creamed chicken and veggies. It'll need some bread with it. Or mashed potatoes." Clara looked up from the dominoes. "Mashed potatoes," she decided.

"Now that's something I *can* do," Artie answered.

"If it comes out of a box…" Clara laughed. "Just keep the casserole in the oven warming until we're ready for supper. That is, if you don't mind me staying."

"Of course not!"

Well, another person to watch over, Boyd thought. Not impossible, of course, but just another moving piece on the chessboard. He *did* enjoy seeing the happiness Clara clearly gave Herman and there was no question that she took pleasure in his company.

Cozy little scene. He went to stare out the front window at the slowly dimming day. A scene he'd never known. A family and a friend who were close and happy together. Had he ever truly tasted that in his adult life? It would be so easy to just settle in with these people and stay.

But darker thoughts haunted him as they'd been haunting him since he'd learned of Linda's assault.

Memories surging from a war, unleashed by the rage he felt toward Linda's attacker. He clenched his fists and reached for his self-control.

Worse, though, he started wondering about Shelley. As little as she would tell him about Linda and how she was doing, why had she called at all to tell him Linda had been raped? Why had she shared that when she'd been doing everything she could to keep Boyd cut out of the picture, even before their divorce?

He closed his eyes, expelling a long breath. Telling him just so he could feel even worse for not being there for Linda, for being an absentee father for so long?

Since that phone call he'd begun to wonder about a lot of things. Trouble was, he wasn't sure of his own reactions, not since PTSD had bitten him on the butt after his last tour. How could he trust himself to be thinking clearly when Afghanistan kept trying to pop up? Trying to take over again?

He wanted to growl in frustration but silenced himself. He didn't want to upset the happy group behind him.

Damn, he needed action. Action of any kind. This waiting crap was going to kill him.

Then he had a thought. Checking his watch, he realized it still wasn't 5:00 p.m. in Seattle. Maybe time to call that attorney he'd used for the divorce. Get some information on just what rights the custody agreement gave him.

Like speaking to his daughter's therapist, to find out how she was really doing.

And whether she had a reason for not wanting to see her father. What were those reasons? Could he help counter them in any way?

He was on this damn trek because he sickened himself enough to want to vomit, because dangerous fury had overwhelmed him. Because he needed to see his daughter and couldn't. Because Shelley had promised to let him know the instant Linda agreed to see him. Because he'd give his life to hug his daughter just once.

Stepping outside into the deepening twilight, hardly aware of the frigid temperature or the growing clouds in the sky, he punched the number on his autodial and turned his back to the street, to break the wind. He hardly heard the truck move down the street behind him. Traffic had become more common throughout the day.

He got the lawyer's receptionist, of course, but she promised the attorney would call the next day, probably after court, mid- to late afternoon.

Good. He shoved his phone back into his pocket and suddenly realized he was close to getting frostbite on his fingertips and nose.

Genius, he thought sarcastically. He knew better. But then he should have known better about a whole bunch of things.

As the light dimmed to almost nothing, Willie and Joe drove their ATV along the icy street past the cop's house. Needed to check on who was there.

They didn't get very close before Joe started swearing a blue streak. "Is some guy livin' with her now?" Joe cussed. "You see him out there without a parka? Ain't no weakling."

"We're heavier than him," Willie reminded him confidently. "Like football players. 'Member, we played us a good game in high school." He didn't much like what he saw, either, but that didn't change nothin'.

"Well, yeah. Maybe. And they's two of us."

"Yup. 'Member how we used to knock them linemen down? Nothin' on us and this one guy ain't *them*."

Then Joe cussed again. "They's having a freakin' party in there! Look at all them people." He added a few more cusswords. The man had gone inside so Willie slowed down and looked. The front windows were uncovered, revealing at least four people inside.

Then he started cussing, too.

"Haveta wait," Joe ranted. "Can't take much more, Willie."

"Me neither."

When they got home, he was gonna call Mack again, even though the guy was nothin' but a heap of warnings. Maybe he'd change his mind a bit and suggest somethin' useful.

Sometimes Willie wondered if Mack had the only smart brain 'tween the three of them. Well, mebbe not so smart. Lost his license after all.

Chapter Thirteen

Dinner, served around the kitchen table, proved to be as delightful as the afternoon had been. Herman was at his best, telling old jokes. Clara smiled and laughed. Artie felt a whole heck of a lot better. Boyd didn't say much, but there was evident warmth in his gaze and a slight smile on his face that made Artie feel even better.

This man deserved far better than the cards he'd been dealt.

In fact, she was starting to feel a little disgusted with herself. All that had happened with Lauer didn't amount to a hill of beans compared to what Boyd had been through.

Hell, he'd probably reckoned with a whole lot more than she could begin to imagine. Had learned to live with it all somehow. Now she needed to stiffen up and do the same.

She'd known when she'd signed up to be a cop that violence could become part of her life. What she hadn't imagined was what she could do, repeatedly, with her own hands. Wonder she hadn't broken his ribs.

Why she thought that was any worse than shooting him, she couldn't quite imagine. Except that she had lost control. Control was the one thing she needed to exert when she was walking around with a pistol on her belt and a riot gun in her vehicle. She'd always exercised it before.

Until Lauer. She wondered how long she was going to be scared of herself. Scared of losing her cool and overreacting.

She sighed and smiled at the conversation and felt little of the warmth inside her. The chill wouldn't quite leave her heart or soul. Not quite.

Despite herself, she glanced at the wall phone and wondered if that episode was over. If the bully who'd made those calls had had his fun and was now done.

God, she hoped so. Looking at her father, she knew she couldn't bear to have anything bad happen to him. To have someone willfully hurt him.

Then she realized that Boyd had looked at the wall phone, too, as if following her gaze and her thoughts. Their eyes met, and she felt a flash of lightning zing between them. Electric desire. Oh, God, she wanted him again.

But there was more, the concern that tightened the corner of his eyes. A strange mixture, she thought, as she saw her hunger briefly reflected in his face, along with that concern for her.

What a mess! Of two minds. Threatened or not threatened? Risk ignoring the threat and have it come true? Or give up on the need she felt, a need that was for normalcy as much as anything.

To be free of this whole chaotic situation and cling to one thing from the rest of life. A good thing. Not all the bad stuff that seemed determined to take over.

The chat around the table continued casually until Artie felt the weight of Boyd's warm hand on her thigh, the light squeeze of his fingers. Her eyes leaped to his and she saw again that slight smile, but this one decidedly warm.

She closed her eyes and released a long sigh. His hand slipped away. Herman's attention jumped to her. "Something wrong, Artie?"

She shook her head. "Maybe something right for once."

The sound of Boyd's quiet laugh eased the chill in her heart.

If he could reach past all his misery, maybe she could, too.

BOYD AND ARTIE took over the cleanup duty, sending Clara and Herman back to the living room recliners. The two of them just couldn't run out of conversation. Happy sounds. Good sounds.

Boyd spoke as he began to wash dishes. "Clara's good for Herman, isn't she? The two of them get along like a house on fire."

Artie nodded, smiling. "I love hearing it, watching it."

"I'm surprised they haven't moved in together."

At that Artie laughed. "Clara's definite about that. She said she was leg-shackled to one man for most of her adult life and likes being able to make all her own decisions without discussion."

Boyd returned her smile. "I can see that. Did she really call it leg-shackled?"

"She did." Artie shook her head and brushed hair back from her face with her forearm. "They were in love, though. She might feel free in some ways, now, but she misses Greg to this day. It just gets quieter with time, I hear."

"The grief? That's what I hear, too. Sometimes I don't believe it, but everyone's different."

The wall phone rang. Artie froze, a plate in her hands, and turned her head to stare at it.

Boyd moved toward it but she stopped him.

"No. If it's the station, they know my cell number and I get caller ID."

"You need caller ID on this phone, too," he remarked, returning to help with the cleanup.

"Until now I never did. I guess it's time to change that."

But as the last dishes and pans were dried and put away, Artie eyed that wall phone. White, slightly yellowed by the years. Remembering how her mother was disappointed to have to switch from the rotary dial to the punch buttons because the old phone had died.

Then, without warning, Boyd's arms slid around her, holding her tightly, astonishing her by lifting her onto the counter so that he stood between her legs.

"Boyd?" But suddenly she could barely find breath to squeeze out that one word.

"Shh," he murmured, running one hand over her

hair while the other arm held her tight. He moved in a little closer, until their centers pressed and she could feel how hard he had grown for her.

"I want you," he said quietly. "At the worst time possible."

Her heart hammering, her breath coming in gasps. Electricity tingling through every inch of her body. Helplessly, she rocked her hips against him, bringing him even closer. "Your timing stinks."

"Right now it does. And they're too busy to notice."

His hand slipped until it cupped her head from behind, then he pressed her lips into his.

No gentle kiss. A hard, demanding one. Feeling as if it would suck the very heart from her. She raised her own arms, wrapping them around his neck, wanting him closer and closer.

Right now nothing seemed close enough, not even his tongue as it speared into her mouth, teasing exquisitely sensitive nerve endings.

Just about the time she grew certain she'd never be able to breathe again and didn't care, he tore his mouth from hers and tucked her head onto his shoulder. A powerful shoulder that smelled good of man, of soap, of the outdoors.

"God, I don't want to let go of you," he said roughly.

"I don't want you to let go," she admitted. Odd to feel so weak and so strong all at once, but that's what he did for her. Weak and strong. A heady sensation.

Reluctantly she drew her arms from around his neck, then ran her hands over his strong back and powerful arms. A protector.

That's what he was built for, whatever he might think, and he'd already made it clear that he wanted to protect her and her father. Strangers to him, but that didn't seem to matter. And maybe they weren't strangers anymore.

But however he'd failed his wife and child, Artie was sure it wasn't because he hadn't tried to protect them. Maybe the Army had kept him away too much. Maybe his wife's decision to remain a thousand miles away with her family instead of knitting a home for herself, Boyd and their baby had had a lot to do with it. There was no way for her to know.

All she knew was the man she leaned into right now, and she didn't think he could possibly be the failure he believed himself to be.

Dang, how many men would walk clear across the country hoping to see their daughter again, all the while lashing themselves with guilt? Not many, she'd bet. Most would have either shrugged it off because they weren't wanted, or would have hopped a plane and arrived in an angry, controlling mood.

Boyd had chosen a better option, she thought. He'd given control to his daughter, who probably desperately needed it after being raped.

She wondered how she could talk to him about that? Could she even persuade him if she did? Was it her place at all?

Then the kitchen phone rang again.

Their eyes met, all softness gone. Boyd stepped back, steadying her as she slid from the counter. She tried not to shake as she took the few steps and reached for the receiver.

"Jackson," she said, the word clipped. Then she heard Guy's voice and relief made her knees weak. As if sensing it, Boyd pushed one of the kitchen chairs over so she could sit.

"It's Guy," she said to Boyd.

He stepped back, leaning against the counter, folding his arms. He appeared far from relaxing completely.

BOYD *WAS* FAR from relaxing. It didn't matter to him that it was Guy, that Artie appeared relieved to hear his voice. The idea that she had weakened upon realizing that it was not another telephone threat told him a hell of a lot more than anything she'd been admitting.

Nor did he think this call was going to be stuffed with cheery news like "we've caught the caller." Not likely.

As he watched, he saw tension creep back into Artie, a tension she'd utterly lost when they embraced just now. The softening, the melting, it all vanished within a minute.

He cussed silently and unfolded his arms, unconsciously preparing himself for trouble. Stiffening into readiness, like when he marched out into enemy territory. His fists clenched and unclenched.

"Thanks, Guy," she said finally. "Just keep updating me, please? And no, I don't need a guard outside. I don't *want* one. I already feel like a prisoner, and frankly I'm going to be more at risk when I leave this house."

Boyd spoke, not caring that he interrupted a supposedly private conversation. "Artie won't be going anywhere alone."

Her head jerked around; the receiver came far enough from her ear that he heard Guy's voice say, "Glad to hear it. That Boyd fellow? You couldn't ask for better."

When Artie disconnected, she glared at Boyd. "You're not going to be my watchdog, either."

"Sure I am. Just try to stop me."

They stared at each other, chins setting stubbornly, then at last Artie dropped her gaze to stare at her hands. They rested on her lap, turned upward, looking relaxed.

Boyd doubted they were relaxed at all. This woman was good at hiding inside herself. Probably made her a good cop, not to reveal herself and her thoughts unnecessarily.

It was also maddening. He wanted to scoop her up again, hug her until she squeaked and promised to start talking.

That would turn him into a hell of a brute. Screw that.

He sighed and leaned back against the counter again. "Okay, I get it. Accepting help mashes your ego. But in this case, nobody is going to let you get *physically* mashed, okay? Like it or not. This Guy sure seems to want to protect you. And from meeting the sheriff, Gage Dalton, I think he pretty much feels the same. Wouldn't surprise me if they keep an eye on you whether you want it or not."

At last she blew a long breath, brushed her black hair back from her face and tucked it behind her ears. When she looked up, he saw just how weary her eyes appeared now. She'd hidden it well, but not now. It was as if she trusted him enough to reveal her exhaustion.

He stepped closer and squatted, taking her hands in his. His right knee objected, a long-ago battle injury, but he never let it stop him. Right now, nothing but a fifty-cal bullet hitting him in the chest could have stopped him.

"Tell me," he said quietly, "a little about this Guy. Redwing, you said at some point?"

She nodded. Almost reluctantly she wound her fingers with his. A small hand in a large hand. "Guy Redwing. Our newest detective. He's Indigenous and I'm sure that's given him some trouble over the years, but he's the best. Kinda stoic, but I'd trust him to have my back in the worst situation."

"Sounds like a good man."

"He is." Her fingers tightened. "Boyd, the department can't afford to put any kind of detail on me. I don't know how much I have to emphasize that, but after this storm everyone's going to be stretched to the limit, more even than usual. People still haven't been able to dig out. They may need food or supplies. They may not have heat or water. Some may have gotten injured." Then she averted her face. "When people get locked up like this, well, domestic violence rises, too. Every man and woman in the department is going to be needed all over this county."

He nodded. "I get that. And like I said, I'm not letting you go anywhere alone."

She released a heavy breath. "And my dad? I can't leave him here alone, not after that phone call."

"Then he'll get some out-and-abouting with us. We'll deal. I'll help you deal. For once, damn it, just take the ego bruising."

That brought the faintest of smiles to her face. "I guess you figured me out."

"It's like reading a book I wrote." He watched the astonishment appear on her face, then a small laugh escaped her.

"God, Boyd, you're something else!"

"We try." He released her hands reluctantly and stood because his knee demanded it and there was no point in annoying it unnecessarily.

"More coffee? Or one of those beers I stuffed in your fridge?"

"Beer," she said after a moment. "I don't need to get any more wound up. I'm doing just fine in that department."

"Or I could get you a brandy?"

She shook her head. "My dad and Clara are having too much fun out there. I don't want to disturb them."

He put two longnecks on the table, and they sat again facing each other. "I'm getting addicted to this table," he remarked, taking a long pull from the bottle.

"No place else right now. I suppose one of these days I should open up the dining room again. It's been closed since Mom died and I just haven't gone in there. Haven't even cleaned or dusted it. She used to make such a big deal of setting a perfect dinner table even for just the three of us. Making it special. It hurts to look in there. But right now I'm wishing for the extra room. You wouldn't have to sleep on the couch."

"I'm fine on the couch."

"And I could offer Clara a place to stay tonight. I don't want her going home alone. Don't ask me why."

Boyd tilted his head. "Then give her your bed, you can take the sofa, and I'll sleep on the rug. Trust me, I've slept in worse conditions. At least there won't be a stubborn rock poking into my ribs."

She smiled at him, sipped her own beer.

Boyd had been letting her find her way past the mood that had struck her during Guy's call, but he couldn't let it go forever. No way. He had to know what disturbed her because it might be important to this entire situation.

"So," he asked slowly, quietly, "what news did Guy have for you?"

Her face sagged. "Nothing, really. They can't identify whoever called me. A burner. They tracked one call to a tower out where the land is so flat the line of sight allows it to work over a huge area. Any number of people out there, some not on the registered deeds. Anyway, they got that one call, then the tower started to fritz. There was another call from a different tower, nearer to town. Again transmission troubles. Storms are good at that. They're still looking.

As for the rest…" She shrugged. "Who knows how many records glitched during the blizzard."

"So there's no way to know who's been bugging you."

"Not yet anyway. Doesn't matter where he, or they, are, I guess. They still have to get to me."

"Well, it doesn't make the situation any worse."

That pulled another smile to her face, a small one. "Man, you're positive."

"You know damn well I'm not always. Anything else?"

"Yeah. Bea's gonna recover. Good news. She's refusing to press charges. Not good."

His head jerked back a bit. "You mean that bastard is going to get off free?"

She shook her head. "The prosecutor is filing the charge anyway. Evidence. They have a record of her injuries and they have me to testify that *he* did it to her."

"So it all comes down to you."

"Evidently."

Boyd sat very still, absorbing the news, trying not to get angry with the victim, waiting for Artie to look at him again.

"Well, that explains a lot. Every reason for you not to testify."

She shrugged. "I told you I will. They can't stop me."

"And as we mentioned at the time, there's only one way to stop you."

"But why the calls, Boyd? Why would they think they could scare me off?"

"Because maybe they don't know diddly about the law."

AFTER THE BEER, they went to the living room, where Clara and Herman appeared content in the separate recliners. Didn't keep them from extending their hands across the side table. Holding hands.

Artie felt a bubble of warmth rise in her. Precious moments for the two of them, well worth protecting.

Clara giggled when she saw them, but she didn't tug her hand out of Herman's.

Artie sat on the couch. "I was thinking, Clara, I'd like you to spend the night here. I'd just feel better about it."

Clara shook her head. "No room at the inn."

"We'll make room. You can have my bed, I'll sleep on the couch and Boyd's offered to sleep on the floor."

Clara eyed Boyd and spoke dryly. "The floor, huh?"

Artie nearly blushed at her obvious subterfuge.

Boyd then startled the room. "Is it anyone's business where I sleep?"

After an instant of surprise, everyone burst into laughter, including Artie.

"Well, it's Artie's business," Clara said archly. "But none of mine or Herman's, right, honey?"

Herman was smiling. "No Artemis anymore, huh?"

"Dang it, Dad!"

He laughed.

"What's that mean?" Clara asked.

"Oh, God, don't ask him that, *please*. Spare me. He just likes to yank my chain."

"Tsk," Clara said to Herman. "Don't be bad to your

daughter." Then she leaned toward Artie's dad. "I'll just ask later anyway."

Artie rolled her eyes, but there was no escaping this. Nor upon reflection did she really want to. A glance at Boyd told her all was good with him, so she let it go.

Then she rose. "Bedtime snacks anyone?"

EVERYONE WAS AGREEABLE to finishing the coffee cake that was in the fridge. Hot cocoa joined it, all of it prepared and served with Boyd's help.

The two older people looked quite delighted to be waited on, especially Clara, who'd probably spent most of her life looking after a family and now taking care of herself. And Artie's dad.

Eventually, though, as the night deepened, Boyd stood, stretching. "I need some air and I need to get a few more logs in here for the fire. I'll be back in a jiff."

Artie watched him pull on his jacket and zip it up, the balaclava going on over his head. She had the very strong feeling that he wasn't going out just for a breath and an armload of wood.

Okay. So this experienced veteran seemed to be more concerned than she was. Or maybe she just wasn't letting herself face it.

IT WAS TRUE Boyd had more on his mind than wood and fresh air. With the town and parts of the county steadily digging themselves out, the opportunities to get to Artie were increasing. He was on a mission, one of reasonable stealth, to hunt for any sign that a human had been prowling. The emerging moon brightened the snow almost to daylight brightness, making it harder to remain unseen.

But the same would hold true for anyone who tried to approach.

Shoveled sidewalks were covered with boot prints now. It looked as if a mail person had been delivering, sometimes approaching front doors. Awful job, he often thought. But those approaches went straight to front doors, then back to the street.

Most people had cleared enough of the snowbanks away to make their cars and doors accessible. Lots of hard work had been happening that day.

But there was little sign of anything untoward nearby. Kids had been playing in yards, trying to build snowmen, but the ground was all trampled, mostly by small feet, and the partial snowmen stood testament to the activity.

At last he began looking around the back. He circled Clara's house first, wanting the snow to be untouched when he reached Artie's, unless someone else had been out there.

Nothing. Pristine snow, muddled a bit from his own trips with the snow shovel, greeted his eyes. No one had come back, at least not here.

Shaking his head, trying to decide how he wanted to evaluate this noninformation, he scooped a huge armload of wood and returned inside through the mud room. The logs had come from lower in the woodpile, from beneath a tarp that had provided some protection, but they still had snow caught on them.

Messy mudroom, he thought with mild amusement as he mopped up the increasing puddle from the wood and his boots.

Then he lifted his head, thinking. Maybe this guy, the one making the threats, didn't need to hurry. Maybe he could afford to take his time.

Well, hell, wouldn't that be just great?

THE LATHROP BROTHERS had given up and started shoveling. Riding their ATV through town had seemed kind of obvious, and cold, too. Besides, there was that party going on in there.

Beer fueled the process, of course, and from time to time they went inside to warm themselves with some whiskey. Maybe even some coffee.

"Shouldn't gotta work this hard," Joe complained.

Willie didn't disagree. "Could drive to Miami."

Joe snorted. "Like that damn truck'd get us there."

With more whiskey the shoveling seemed less important. Besides, it was warm in front of the fire, and comfy in them old recliners their bodies had mashed into shape over the years.

"Still ain't figgered it out," Willie said finally. "That damn cop gonna be the death of me."

"More likely *me*," Joe groused.

"Worse can happen."

The two brothers glared at each other and appeared ready to come to blows, but then another pour of whiskey and they settled back.

Willie spoke. "At least we gotta look-see."

"Yeah," Joe retorted. "And that guy ain't no twig."

"Anyway," Willie continued. "He don't look like no football player. We got the edge on that, 'member?"

Joe relaxed a bit. "Yeah, we got the moves."

"Tackle good, don't we?"

"Allus."

"That's it. He ain't no problem. Take 'im out, then we get to that cop, and mebbe her damn dad."

"Whadda we want him for? Old guy just get in the way."

"Hostage," said Willie. "Make her do what we want."

At that Joe finally looked appalled. "Things ain't bad enough the way they is?"

Chapter Fourteen

Night blanketed the house, bringing the utter quiet of a town fallen into sleep. Boyd lay on the rug beneath a blanket Artie had found somewhere, using his jacket for a pillow. His gaze followed the flicker of firelight on the ceiling and he dozed on and off. Experience had taught him to sleep like a cat. At a single sound he could wake instantly, be ready.

He hadn't even taken off his boots, because if there was one thing a soldier knew, it was that when you had to hit the ground, your feet needed protection.

He was comfortable in his old gray sweats, though. As he listened, he could hear Artie's quiet, steady breathing. Reassuring. And if he'd had to bet on it he'd have taken odds that Clara was sharing Herman's bed.

The thought made him smile faintly. A bit of pleasure did everyone some good. Life offered little enough of it.

No unusual sounds disturbed him, though. Not a one. The sounds of the old house had become familiar, almost reassuring. Nothing different there.

The fire was dying down, but still splashed flame and light. Cozy.

Maybe not cozy enough. His thoughts kept wandering to Artie, wondering what he was getting into with her. If she'd allow him to get into anything at all.

And Linda. She remained his priority. Maybe he'd hear from the damn lawyer tomorrow with some good news. He could sure use some.

Then, a while later, he felt Artie's hand brush his arm. Probably fell off the couch while she slept, he thought.

But then her hand began to move in a light unmistakable caress. In one mere instant he burned hotter than any fire.

"Artie?" he whispered. "You awake?"

Her answer was to slide off the couch until she rested on top of him.

Oh, Lord, fireworks exploded in his head.

"Boyd," she breathed, then their mouths met in a kiss that was far from gentle. Hunger filled it with strength. A sealing of breaths together.

His arms wrapped around her, holding her crushingly tight. Had he ever wanted a woman this much? If so, he couldn't remember it. She writhed against him, blanket and clothing creating a maddening barrier.

"Boyd," she murmured again when their mouths separated and breath returned. "I need…"

So did he. No time for finesse, though. Not here plain as day on this damn floor when either Clara or Herman could rise for a glass of water.

Boyd lifted her slightly and yanked the blanket

away. He found the waistband of her pajama bottoms and tugged them down. Then his own sweatpants. Heat met heat, so sweet, so exciting, crazing.

He found his way into her hot depths, then slipped his hands beneath the blanket, hoping they weren't cold, and cupped her breasts, finding her puckered nipples.

The softest of moans escaped her as she started rocking against him. He bit back his own groans of pleasure and let her take the lead. She'd taken the bit between her teeth and rode him hard, then harder. A lighting storm erupted in his head, driving away everything except the miracle of Artie.

Then soon, way too soon, completion found them, weakening them with total satisfaction. Artie lay limply on him and he could barely move enough to tug the blanket over them, concealing them, warming them even more.

"God," Artie murmured, keeping her voice low. "God, Boyd. You ignite me."

"Same here," he said a bit gruffly. "You set me off like a range fire."

The quietest laugh escaped her. "Maybe you're the best thing that's walked into my life in a while."

"Ditto." He meant it, too. She took him out of himself, carried him to nicer places, places he wanted to reach and remain eventually. She didn't make him forget, but she offered the possibility of better things to come.

Not necessarily with her, he reminded himself. She sure seemed determined to remain self-sufficient.

She might well feel that she had enough on her plate without taking on a vet with a passel of problems that seemed to dog his every step.

She had a pretty normal life as near as he could tell. A normalcy he'd never known, not even in his broken childhood home.

But none of that kept him from enjoying these precious minutes while she relaxed on him, sighing quietly, occasionally running a hand over his arm or shoulder. Moments like these should be eternal.

Eventually, Artie raised her head. "I suppose I should get back on the couch."

Boyd snorted quietly. "As if Herman doesn't already know or suspect."

"But Clara…"

"I'd bet ten bucks right now that she's in bed with him."

A soft titter escaped Artie. "I sometimes wonder what those two get up to when I'm working."

"Wouldn't surprise me if it's more than dominoes. You see how they look at each other."

About like Boyd was looking at Artie these days. About like she'd begun to look at him.

"Yeah." She sighed. "It's so good for him."

Good for him, too, Boyd thought, but didn't say so. He had no right to push the issue, not given his other problems.

But reality returned because it always did. Because it *had* to.

Artie spoke quietly. "You said something about calling a lawyer?"

"She's supposed to get back to me tomorrow."

He felt Artie nod against his chest. "You've got to have *some* rights."

"At least to find out the truth from Linda's counselor, not just what Shelley wants to tell me."

"This must hurt like hell."

"It does." Why not admit it? There were all kinds of pain and grief in life, but this one was taking the cake, even more so because he couldn't evade his own responsibility, his own failures as a father. Maybe he had no right to happiness at all.

But he had a right to know how his daughter was doing. How she was coping. If she'd ever want a hug from him.

Then he thought he heard something from outside.

He eased Artie to the side. "I heard something," he said quietly. "Stay here. Keep an eye on your father."

In one, swift easy movement he rose to his feet, pulled on his parka and watch cap, then slipped silently out the front door.

Sitting in a heap of blankets, Artie stared after him, her heart racing. Then she rose swiftly and went to her bedroom. As they'd suspected, Clara wasn't in there. Which made it easier for Artie to unlock her pistol and grab her baton.

If anyone came into this house tonight, they were going to meet hell unbound.

ACROSS THE STREET, mostly hidden behind the huge ancient trunk of an elm tree, probably one of the very few on this continent that had escaped the ravages of

Dutch elm disease, Mack Murdo watched. He had to figure out a way out of this heap of crap Joe and Willie was busy building. He'd tossed a small rock across the street at the side of the cop's house, and now waited for a reaction.

He saw the guy come out the front door, as if he'd reacted. Murdo was pretty sure he'd been soundless, other than the rock, but neither his hearing nor his eyesight were as good as they'd been in his hunting days.

He didn't really have a horse in this race, other than his friendship with Billy Lauer. Good drinking buddies from way back. He didn't much care about Joe Lathrop at all. Man was a stupid sucker. But it might do Mack some good to see that bitch of a cop get her comeuppance.

Now Mack, frankly, didn't want to deal with killing that woman and he was getting a notion that the Lathrops were thinking about it. Nor did he like the idea that the Lathrop boys had threatened the old man. A coward's choice.

Mack Murdo had *some* standards. His grievance didn't reach killing or taking people as hostages.

But he *did* give a damn about Billy Lauer. Man had beat his wife. So what? Men did that. Gotta keep a woman in line. But not to the extent of nearly killing the woman or getting an attempted murder charge for it.

Whether the Lathrop boys wanted to listen to his cousin the lawyer didn't matter. They didn't freaking get the whole picture.

So while Mack Murdo wanted to teach that cop a lesson, he wanted no part of the Lathrops' messy plans. Not to that kind of extent.

And to make matters worse, they'd called the woman and threatened her father. What good did they think that would do? The few words of sense he'd tried to push their way had gone unheeded or unheard.

Nothing like those two to get obsessed.

Mack was a guy who preferred to take his time when he could. Those two hadn't waited for anything except a blizzard. And their own lack of a plan.

He watched the stranger examine the street, look around, hike toward the back of the house.

Guy was on watch, no doubt of that. None at all.

Skinny or not, something in the way he moved bothered Mack. He could be a threat. A real threat, for which neither of the Lathrops would be prepared. Or even able to handle.

Then there was that cop herself. She'd beat Billy near to death, he'd heard. Except she hadn't put Billy in the hospital. Lucky Billy. He wondered if the Lathrop boys had gotten the measure of that. What that woman might do if her family was threatened.

Mack bit back a sigh and waited, watching. Too many people in that house right now anyway, according to what Joe and Willie had told him. Needed to get the numbers down.

The stranger came round again to the front of the house, surveyed the street, then returned inside.

Okay then. Mack started shambling down the side-

walk, trying to appear aimless, but he wasn't aimless
at all.

Hell, no. He was going to talk some good sense
into those boys, then try to get them to make a plan
that wouldn't get any of them killed or maimed. And
still teach that cop a lesson.

He didn't much care if the Lathrops went to prison,
but he damn well wasn't going himself. Which might
mean knocking Joe's and Willie's heads together.

Mack shook his head and let an exasperated growl
escape him. How the hell had it come to this? Simply because he'd sympathized about the cop. Had he
dragged himself into this by being a friend?

Some friends the Lathrops had turned out to be.
Heads as thick as blocks of cement, hearing everything wrong.

Everything.

ONCE INSIDE, Boyd saw Artie at the ready, collapsed
baton in her hand, service pistol belted to her side.
Every line of her was poised for action.

He tried to keep the snow on his boots to the rug in
front of the door, saying, "Nothing. No one's been out
there. Must have been a branch or something caught
by the wind."

Muscle by muscle she relaxed, almost as if unwilling to let go of her preparedness, almost as if she
needed to act.

He understood that. This waiting for a threat to
materialize wasn't sitting well with him, either.

Artie finally uncoiled and began to unbelt her pistol. "Coffee," she said presently.

He had to agree. As much as he'd enjoyed their lovemaking, as much as he wanted to stay cocooned in that blanket with her, neither of them was in the mood any longer.

Tension had invaded and wasn't going to leave them anytime soon.

Before long they sat at the kitchen table, hot mugs of coffee between them.

"I need to make some more bread," Boyd remarked absently.

"That was sure good." She sounded about as enthusiastic as he felt.

Between them on the table lay her baton and pistol. A reminder. No escaping it.

She raised a weary face. "I sure as hell wish I had any kind of clue about who's behind this."

"The wife beater is still in jail?"

"Until tomorrow, at least."

"Then?"

"Then Judge Carter will arraign him. Maybe give him bail."

"A man like that? With what he's done?" That seriously troubled Boyd.

Artie shook her head. "Among other things, bail has to be reasonable for the crime. At this point I don't know what the prosecutor will charge him with. Or be able to charge him with. Right now all Amberly has to go on is my brief description from the scene and

Bea Lauer's condition. I'll need to make a statement eventually, but right now?" Artie shrugged.

"So what exactly will happen?"

"Amberly will go to court and present the charges. Lauer will be given an opportunity to plead. He'll plead not guilty of course. Then both Amberly and Lauer's lawyer will argue terms of bail. It's all up to the judge in the end."

Boyd nodded and reached across the table to touch her hand. "Which is ripping you up?"

"No. It's standard. The only things ripping me up are my own conduct at the Lauer scene and the threat against my dad."

He breathed a curse. "What do you think of this judge?"

One corner of her mouth tipped up. "An honest man who really gives a damn about the cases that come before him. I admire and respect him. He never just runs by the book."

Then she snorted.

"What?"

"The judge's father is Earl Carter, one of our local lawyers. Wouldn't it be something if he got tapped to be the public defender for Lauer?"

Boyd's head jerked up a bit. "Wouldn't that be a conflict?"

"Who knows? Earl is as respected as his son. Honest as the day is long. I guess the only one who might object would be the judge himself. Then comes the question of who else they can tap. Not that many criminal defense lawyers around here. They might have to bring someone in from outside the county. That'd gum up the works."

Boyd nodded, taking in all the complexities, but mildly amused that they were talking about the legalities and avoiding the one thing foremost on both their minds.

But what else could they do? Nothing was more anxiety-inducing than to have no gauge of the threat. Of where it might come from. Running blind into a possible narrow defile, as he had so many times. Wondering who was on top of those cliffs or if anyone was there at all.

Artie spoke suddenly. "You know what I'm never going to forgive? This bastard threatening my father." She slipped her hand from beneath his and balled it into a tight fist.

"I completely understand."

"I'm sure you do." Then she shook her head. "Damn it, Boyd, I'm feeling that violence rising in me again. The same thing that happened when I beat Billy Lauer with my baton. I hate feeling like I can kill."

"But anyone can," he said flatly. "*Anyone* can kill in the right circumstances, and saving a life or protecting family…those are some of the circumstances."

She sighed, blowing the breath straight up her face so that it ruffled her feathery bangs. "I'm starting to hate myself."

"Oh, for Pete's sake," he said sharply. "Don't do that. You have no reason to. Think about it. Lauer had beaten his wife to a pulp and was strangling the life from her. That's what you said. What else were you supposed to do? Hold up a peace sign? You said he wouldn't listen, his wife was on the brink of death and there was only one thing you could do. *Get his attention.* Break his focus and intent. In the process you might have gotten yourself killed."

She closed her eyes. "Maybe."

"No maybe about it. Take it from me. I've been there. And that kind of incident is one of the few that never gives me nightmares. Never. Much as we may dislike it, there are situations that justify that kind of reaction."

"I don't know." She sighed again.

"Think about it. If you feel bad now, how would you have felt if Lauer had succeeded in killing his wife while you stood helplessly by?"

Her head lifted, her blue eyes glistening just a bit. "I didn't think of it that way."

"Of course not. You're a nice, moral, law-abiding person. You broke all three of those parts of yourself. Hard to deal with."

"Broken," she murmured. "That's how I feel." The description cut her to the bone.

"You won't always feel that way, not to this degree. You'll find your footing again."

One corner of her mouth quirked. "Have *you*?"

"A lot more than I had when I came home for the last time."

She didn't answer him, sat there lost in thought.

Then, surprising him, she jumped up and started looking through the fridge. "God, I'm hungry. Cinnamon rolls? They need to be baked."

"I'll help."

As he stood, she faced him again, and something in her face had softened. She asked quietly, "Is that what you're doing on this hike of yours? Finding your footing?"

He nodded, revealing more of himself than he truly liked, but feeling he needed to share part of his innermost self with this woman. "Yeah. That's some of it. Lots of time to think. To deal with things, like the past, like the dark fog of the future. Like the rage I feel about what happened to Linda. Sooner or later, I gotta deal with it all."

Astonishing him, she put down the tube of rolls and walked straight into his arms. "You're a good buddy," she murmured into his shoulder. "A good friend. We'll both get through this, won't we?"

"We will," he answered with more surety than he felt. "We will."

Chapter Fifteen

Morning arrived cloaked in beauty. The snow gleamed and glistened whitely under the sun, the crystals acting like prisms in some places, reflecting the colors of the rainbow. A sight that might be missed by those who believed that snow was only white.

But it was not. It was full of color.

Artie stood looking out at it, thinking how perfect it was. There hadn't even been enough activity yet to gray the white with blown dust or the exhaust of cars or the woodsmoke that rose from many houses, like her own.

Pristine. Unlike the world that was seriously beginning to stir out there. Kids heading to school. People driving to work. Others shoveling, probably with more than a few curses. Down the street a snowblower shredding the silence with its engine.

She couldn't help smiling, even though she knew what lay behind that perfection. Even though she knew the dark depths that lurked below, that to some extent belonged to all human beings. Even though she awaited action from the man who had warned her to forget, had suggested her father might be at risk. One way or another, something bad lurked, and that bad thing would arrive.

All she could do was prepare mentally and emotionally.

From the kitchen came the aromas of baking cinnamon rolls. Clara had taken over out there, in Herman's company. For the moment anyway, the two had become inseparable.

Clara said something to Herman about needing to go home for a change of clothes. Herman objected. Clara responded that he didn't want to smell her in dirty clothes.

"I'll take you covered with mud," he replied.

Again, Artie smiled.

Boyd, near the kitchen, spoke. "I'll run next door and get whatever you need, Clara. Just give me a list."

"And have you pawing around my underthings?"

Herman chuckled. Boyd's response was dry. "As if I haven't seen any of it before."

"You read lingerie catalogs, do you?"

Both Boyd and Herman guffawed.

A wider smile came to Artie's face, but along with it came apprehension. She didn't like the idea that Clara might be caught in the approaching threat. Didn't like it at all.

But she also didn't know what to do about it. Throwing Clara out, however gently she did it, might cause a serious storm of another kind, mostly with Herman. She couldn't bear the thought of her dad being angry with her.

It wasn't as if it hadn't happened in the past, all the way back to her childhood, but now was different. Very different. God help her if they had a fight and Herman keeled over before she could make amends. Yeah, such morbid thoughts troubled her from time to time. Thoughts she could hardly stand.

EARLY AFTERNOON, the county went into a near state of shock. People in outlying areas were still trying to dig out when another blizzard marched in.

Artie watched heavily falling snow through the window and cussed. Loudly enough to be heard.

Boyd came to stand beside her. "Again?"

"Yeah. This is unreal. Make Clara give you that list. I am *not* sending her home tonight in this."

"I'll make a fast trip to the grocery, too. Did I do okay last time?"

"You did a wonderful job." She turned around to face him. "Boyd, I can't leave them alone here. Not now. Do you mind doing this by yourself?"

He gave her a half smile. "I wouldn't allow you to leave them alone."

She reached in her jeans pocket and handed him keys. "My personal vehicle. It's parked beside my official one."

He nodded. "I'll be fast."

It didn't take Clara long to agree to giving Boyd a list of what she needed. She saw what was coming, too, and clearly didn't want to spend another blizzard alone in her house.

Herman turned on the weather channel. A cheerful meteorologist chatted about the unexpected blizzard and the reasons for it.

Clara spoke. "Have you ever noticed how much these guys enjoy a good weather catastrophe?"

Artie had to laugh, whatever her other worries. "It's their bread and butter. Nobody would watch if the forecast was always for perfect days."

Boyd left swiftly, and with amazing speed returned with Clara's things packed in the suitcase she'd told him about. She thanked him profusely, but before she finished he was out the door again.

Artie heard her car start without a problem. One thing not to worry about.

But another blast of Arctic air had escaped. The stratosphere and the troposphere, whatever they were, had messed up the polar vortex. Look out folks.

Six inches of fresh snow, winds at gale force. Artie wanted to collapse in a chair. *More?*

Even worse, it might prolong the threat, hold it off. More waiting to find out the worst. *Damn it all to hell!*

MACK WAS MORE than ticked by the time he got back to his ramshackle house. Another storm? And those Lathrops so eager to deal with that damn cop that they kept making stupid phone calls and hinting at worse? Now the new storm might make them even more impatient.

And likely to die from the elements before they even got near that Jackson woman. Somehow he had to figure out an idea that would keep them all from getting life sentences but settle those two jackasses down enough that there wasn't a string of bodies halfway across the county.

But one thing was for sure. He wasn't going anywhere near those two blockheads. In no way did he want to be considered abetting whatever they did. It was stupid of him to have ever thought that suggesting a phone call would palliate them. Give them chuckles the way they'd shared during their school days by making nuisance calls.

Nope. These jerks had turned this all into a steamroller, and nothing he'd said had slowed it down.

WILLIE AND JOE were having their own thoughts about the coming storm and they weren't silent ones. Joe cussed a blue streak, not very inventive because he only knew some basic cuss words.

Willie threw a bottle of beer across the room. Beer washed everywhere but the bottle didn't break, which was good because neither of them was going to waste time cleaning up broken glass. As for the beer, it didn't matter. Whole place reeked of it along with woodsmoke and unwashed bodies. They were nose blind.

"What now?" Joe demanded. "I ain't gonna wait forever. Dang, we should call Billy, see if he's outta jail yet."

"What's he s'posed to do?"

"*Help!* Mack ain't being much help."

"He don't really want no part of this. Been mad at us since we made the second phone call."

Joe nodded. "Guess so. Said it was a warning to the bitch."

"We was trying to scare her."

"Ain't seen her running yet."

Willy shook his head and grabbed another beer. "Now she got all them people in that damn house. Might be too many even for us." He looked down at his lineman's belly. At least that's how he thought of it.

"Gotta do it anyway," Joe said harshly. "Before we get stuck and can't move again. So think, you bastard. You allus say you got the brain."

Willie had begun to doubt it but refused to say so. He still didn't have a plan, which wasn't making him feel all that smart. "Call Mack."

"What the hell for? He keeps telling us reasons this ain't no good."

"Call 'im anyway. Mebbe he got some idea."

Turned out Mack's only idea was to leave the bitch alone. They'd already gone too far.

Willie and Joe exchanged glances. The words escaped simultaneously. "We gotta kill the broad."

WHEN BOYD RETURNED from the grocery with a trunkful of food, everyone helped put it away. Plenty for another siege.

Then Clara and Herman settled in the living room with the TV still on the weather channel, and Boyd and Artie went to the kitchen for a little privacy. Boyd even started another loaf of bread. That machine sure made a lot of noise.

Artie faced him over the inevitable cups of coffee.

"I have to do something, Boyd. I can't sit here waiting and wondering if those calls were from a bully
or if they were serious. I've had enough of sitting on
tenterhooks, enough of waiting for a bomb or a fire-
cracker. Or nothing at all."

He nodded, his expression grave. "I hear you."

"And with another storm, we'll be locked down
again, wondering. If they're really gonna act, don't
you think it would be soon, before everything becomes impassable again?"

He nodded again. "That's what I would do. But
they're not me."

Artie heaved a big sigh. "No, they're not. I keep
thinking that if those phone calls were genuine threats
then they must be fools. They put me on guard."

"True." He sipped coffee, then drummed his fingers on the table. "But you said the guy wanted you
to forget. Forget what?"

"Something I saw, and I have a pretty good idea.
Intent is important in a murder charge. Right now
Amberly doesn't feel he has enough for attempted
murder. More evidence needed, I guess, although
where he's going to get it from I can't imagine."

"You," Boyd said flatly. "You saw most of it. You
can testify that beast wouldn't quit."

Artie sighed again. "Yeah." The memories surged
to the forefront, making her stomach turn over. "He'll
want my full, formal statement before he can go ahead,
I guess. At least Bea Lauer is safe in the hospital."

Silence fell. More coffee was poured.

Then Artie said, "I need to make myself an easy

target before this storm hits full force. Then if this guy really wants to act, he'll have an opportunity before the whole county gets shut down again."

Boyd's face darkened and he reached across the table, squeezing her hand tightly. "Artie…"

"I need this resolved, Boyd. Somehow. This just can't keep up."

"What if he never shows?"

"Then I'll assume the calls were bullying and I'll get back to normal life."

His hand tightened even more. "And if he does show? Your life may be at risk."

"I know." Her own face darkened. "But, Boyd, I'm a cop. If I'm afraid to face danger, then I should turn in my uniform."

"Well, I can hardly disagree with you about that, considering how many years I spent in uniform."

She offered a crooked smile. "In much more dangerous situations. I'm up against one guy, not an army."

"You assume it's one guy."

She closed her eyes a moment. "I doubt it could be very many."

BOYD COULDN'T ARGUE THAT, EITHER. He totally understood her need to finish this. The storm had created a cocoon in which to be nervous, but not to be truly fearful.

Now there was a break in the weather and any true fear could no longer be quelled. He also understood her need to get this settled before the world became frozen in place once more.

He turned his head, looking out the kitchen window. The snow fell, but not heavily. The worst was supposed to arrive tomorrow. A narrow window in which to take any kind of action.

He faced her again. "You got a plan?"

"I have to be alone. Clara and my dad have to go to her house. You have to head out. The motel, the truck stop diner, anywhere that makes it appear you've moved out."

He gave her a half smile. "I've really moved in?"

"It's beginning to look like it." But her tone was mildly humorous.

He waited a minute, certain he was about to stir up a hornet's nest. Then he said, "I'll come back because I sure as hell am not going to leave you here alone."

"But he might see you!"

Boyd shook his head. "I know how to be surreptitious. Better than this bastard ever will. But I'm not leaving you alone and you'd better get used to it."

Her blue eyes sparked with anger. "I don't want any interference."

"I won't interfere. I want this finished as much as you do." His own irritation was rising. Part of him admired this woman's stubbornness, but he also didn't want to see it turn into foolishness.

"Then why even tell me you'll come back," she snapped. "How could I stop you anyway?"

"Because," he said levelly, "I will never lie to you."

She drew a sharp breath, then her face started to soften and the anger left her gaze. "Boyd…"

"I mean it. There were things I didn't tell you at

the outset because you were a stranger. I just left them unsaid. You did the same, didn't you?"

She nodded.

"But neither of us had lied and now that I know you so well, I'd be lying by omission if I didn't tell you what I'm going to do."

"Oh, Boyd," she murmured softly.

"And I'll thank you to save that tone of voice for a better time."

At least he got a small laugh from her.

Then she said, "The only question is whether it's enough to make the house look empty of everyone except me, or whether I need to get outside."

"After dark," he said presently. "He'll move after dark for the concealment. But he may be watching right now, so we'll move Clara and Herman while it's bright, and I'll leave then, too."

"But later…" She nodded. "After dark. Maybe I'll try a walk to the grocery if the weather isn't too bad. I'll think about it. But first to clear the house."

Chapter Sixteen

Mack had refused to talk to the brothers, so the two numbskulls, as Mack had called them before hanging up, set out for town while the roads were still passable enough.

Tonight, they promised each other. They'd shut up that woman's yap before she could do any more damage. Then hightail it before the storm could freeze them in town. How they were supposed to accomplish this miracle when she had a houseful of people, they didn't know.

But fueled by beer, they believed the fates would favor them. A little stakeout to start, make sure she no longer had a houseful of people. Yeah.

JUST BEFORE ARTIE managed to devise an explanation that could get Clara and her father to move next door, Boyd's cell phone rang.

Since he was now trying to be invisible as possible from watchers outside, he took the call in the kitchen.

A woman's voice spoke. "Mr. Connor? This is Deborah Wainsmith, your attorney. My clerk passed on your questions to me. Do you have a moment?"

Boyd's heart sped up until he thought it would leap from his chest, and he plopped down hard on one of the kitchen chairs. He was hardly aware that Artie watched him.

"Thank you for calling, Ms. Wainsmith."

"Well, I'll charge for the time," she said humorously. "Always."

"Of course." *Get to the point*, he thought impatiently even as he dreaded more bad news.

"I did some research into custody issues for you. You know your ex-wife allowed you to have joint custody, although I'm not sure why, given the way she's been acting. For example, she didn't have the right to take Linda out of the legal state of residence you both shared at the time of the divorce, not without your permission."

Boyd drew a sharp breath. "Honestly?"

"I'm going to call this my fault that you didn't know. I'm sure I must have told you, but you were so upset at the time you may not have taken it all in. I should have made a point of ensuring you understood."

Shelley had had no right to take Linda to Seattle. The realization hit him like a sledgehammer. And if she hadn't taken Linda to Seattle… Boyd couldn't finish the thought.

He cleared his throat. "Anything else?"

"Oh, yes. She has no right to keep you from seeing your daughter. She has no right to exclude you from the counseling sessions."

"Oh, my God," he whispered.

"I've already called Linda's counselor and made her aware of that. If she doesn't call you to give you a report, call me. I'll take care of it."

"And Linda?" All of a sudden everything inside him turned into a block of fearful ice.

"She hasn't expressed any objection at all to seeing you, Mr. Connor. Your ex-wife has been lying."

Boyd squeezed his eyes shut and for the first time in years a tear trailed down his face. "I've been praying," he said thickly.

"Your prayers have been answered. If you want to raise a civil case over this, I will. But if you're happy with knowing the truth, I won't. Just tell me when you make up your mind. And *I* am going to warn your ex that she's crossed some serious legal lines."

When Boyd hung up, he still couldn't open his eyes. His hands shook, whether with gratitude or anger he couldn't have said. Linda wanted to see him. Shelley had been lying.

Oh, God!

Suddenly strong arms wrapped around his shoulders, hugging him tightly. Fingers ran through his hair. "Boyd. Boyd?"

He lowered his head. "I can see Linda," he whispered. "I can see Linda."

ARTIE FELT AS if a hole had torn her heart, but it was a good hole. A hole that had earlier been full of pain had filled now with joy for Boyd. He could see his daughter. As far as she'd been able to determine that had been his primary concern on his trek across the country.

Yeah, he felt as if he'd failed as a father. Maybe he hadn't been around enough because of the Army, but the sense of failure had to come from his daughter refusing to see him. And most of his pain and guilt had arisen from that.

Now he should be free of all that, if he could work his way out of a mental state that had obsessed him for weeks now. He would, she decided. This man had worked his way through a lot of terrible things. He'd find his way now, though it might take time.

She murmured, "So you want to grab a flight out of here as soon as this storm passes? Admittedly, all we have are puddle jumpers…"

He straightened abruptly, causing her to let go of him, and dashed a hand across his face. When he spoke, his voice was like steel.

"I am not moving one inch from here until I'm sure you're safe."

Wow! She straightened, too. This guy wanted so desperately to see his daughter and now he was going to stay for *her* sake?

"Boyd, I can take care of myself. You go to your daughter."

He turned from the waist, his head at her breast level, and stared straight up into face. His eyes looked hard.

"I don't want to hear that anymore."

Startled, she asked, "What?"

"That you can take care of yourself. I get it, Artie.

You're a powerful, strong woman. You're also stubborn as hell. But here's the thing. I'm sure you can take care of yourself in most circumstances. Not a doubt in my mind."

"But?"

"But you don't know what *these* circumstances are. You don't know how many people might come after you. You don't know *how* they might come after you. What if some guy with a damn deer rifle decides to take a shot at you through a window?"

She stiffened. "There's no way on God's earth anyone can prevent that, Boyd."

"Yeah, there is. *I* can. I'm not going to be indoors with you. I'm going to be out there watching anything that stirs where it shouldn't. Yeah, you can take care of yourself, but you don't have two sets of eyes."

"Damn it!" She turned away, inexplicably angry because she knew he was right. She *did* need his eyes.

"What's more," he said, "you're going to tell Herman why you want him over at Clara's. No fishy stories. The man may have Alzheimer's but he's not stupid. He won't argue, bet on it. Because the thing he most wants is for you to be safe, and he'll know that at his age there won't be much he can do. As long as you're not alone."

It was Artie's turn to look down. She grabbed the edge of the counter, squeezed her eyes shut, and faced the truth. Boyd was right. "Okay. Okay."

"WILL YA LOOK at that," Willie said to Joe, who was busily downing a bag of potato chips.

"What?" Joe asked.

"See? The old man and the old woman is goin' next door. They's not gonna be in the house."

"If they stay over there. And there's still the guy." Joe, getting frustrated with this endless watching from a cold, battered pickup just around the corner from the cop's house, reached around to grab another beer from the case behind them.

"The guy," Willie said firmly, "is gonna be up against us two. Plus, it'll be dark. Ain't no one gonna see us comin'."

Joe downed half a bottle of beer.

"Hey, lookee," Willie said with satisfaction. "The jerk is leavin', too. Got his backpack on."

"We ain't called again," Joe remarked. "Mebbe she ain't scared no more."

Willie thought that might be true. Mebbe Mack had been right all this time. He almost hated Mack for that.

THE HOUSE HAD never felt so vacant to Artie before, not even when her father had gone to the senior center with Clara. Boyd's absence left a new kind of emptiness, one that made her almost sad.

She watched him hike away down the street, then pulled all the window curtains closed, casting the house into near darkness. She wondered how many times she might have to do this before the bad guy showed up. Then she reminded herself that they had concluded this would be the only opportunity for days to come because of the steadily arriving storm.

It *had* to be today. The worry about her father far

exceeded any worry about herself. At least he was next door with Clara, and Boyd had assured her he'd keep watch over both houses and the surrounding area.

She believed he could. How many times had he needed to do the same thing in the war? If anyone knew how, *he* did.

When the kitchen wall phone rang, she hesitated before answering it. What if it was another threat? Just an empty one, maybe.

But no, it was Gage Dalton. "How goes it?" he asked Artie.

"Wound up tighter than a drum."

He made a sound deep in his throat. "Do you have a plan?"

She outlined it for him swiftly.

"Good. I agree that if anything's going to happen other than nasty phone calls it'll have to be tonight. Otherwise the creep might get snowed in for a few more days."

"Right." Her hand grew tighter around the receiver. "Gage, I don't want…"

"Yeah, I know. You don't want protection. I get it. And you're going to get your wish, to a point. You know I checked Boyd Connor out and he's all the close-up protection you could ask for, want it or not. But here's the thing. You're not going to be alone, the two of you. I'm going to have some plainclothes out there at a distance watching approaches to your street and alley. Through binoculars, so don't yell at me."

"As if anyone yells at Sheriff Gage Dalton," she managed to say dryly.

He chuckled. "Been known to happen. Anyway, nobody can be sure it's just one creep after you. If someone wants to prevent you from testifying, there could be more than one. And that's your fault for being one of my best cops."

She almost smiled. "Flatterer. You know that's not true."

Gage sighed. "Well, I don't keep useless folks, it's true. Don't have a big enough budget to carry deadweight. Anyhow, if you can contact Boyd about my stakeout, it'll save him a lot of time wondering about the wrong people. If he wants exact locations, have him call me, hear?"

"Will do." She disconnected, once again feeling warm about the sheriff. About most of her colleagues, in fact.

BOYD WAS HIKING back toward the house, keeping to out-of-the way locations, armed with nothing but the Ka-Bar he'd carried for two decades, the one he'd carried cross-country because you never knew, especially when you started to get into real bear territory.

But it had been a while since he'd needed to use it on another human being. He hoped tonight wouldn't break the peace he'd made with himself and the war, imperfect as it was.

When his phone buzzed with Artie's call, he drew behind a thick, snow-covered evergreen and answered.

She explained quickly.

"Okay, I'll call the sheriff. Text me his number. I'll thank him for the heads-up, too. Smart man."

"Nobody ever claimed he was a fool."

"Stay alert, Artie. I feel it coming."

"How can you?"

"Been doing it for a while. I'm going dark now. No incoming calls. I'll phone Dalton now."

He hated going dark because it would prevent Artie from reaching him if she needed help. But there was no choice. A sound from his phone could give him away. Could send this creep and any of his accomplices into flight. No good. This whole thing needed to be done and over so Artie and her father would be safe.

Nothing else mattered. He called Dalton, got the locations of the stakeout, then let the sheriff know where he was and his planned approach. No point causing any confusion on either side.

Then he slipped slowly shadow to shadow among hedges and trees. The bastard would come as soon as he felt he wouldn't be seen by anyone on the streets. Late.

He glanced at his watch. There was plenty of time.

Joe wasn't happy with the continued wait. "It's dark now," he whined.

"You blockhead, it ain't dark enough. We gotta wait til nobody be lookin' out a window or walking on the street."

Joe cussed and pulled out another beer. Stash was gettin' low, which bothered him some. Damn truck felt like being inside an ice cube because Willie insisted they couldn't run the engine without drawing attention.

Maybe Willie was the real blockhead between 'em. Satisfied with that, Joe settled down again.

MACK MURDO, miles safely away, stewed over his own beer, knowing tonight was the night his jackass buddies were going to get themselves into big-time trouble. Joe might only have gotten three or six months for a barroom brawl. Now he was flirting with the rest of his life. So was Willie, come to that.

And Mack wanted to be nowhere near them when it happened. Nope. But he sure would have liked to hog-tie them two lunks to chairs. Maybe for his *own* good. They'd made too many phone calls after all. Sendin' up a flare for that cop.

Jerks. Screaming damn fools.

He stewed some more.

"OKAY," SAID WILLIE FINALLY. "Another hour."

"Hour?" Joe shouted.

"Shut the hell up. You want someone to hear we're in this truck?"

Joe quieted. "I want *out* of this damn truck."

"Soon, you jerk. Soon. Never had two brain cells to rub together."

It was something their mother used to say, mostly to Joe. Occasionally she added Willie, but not as often. Either way, it had always made Joe shrink more than him.

BOYD, NEARING ARTIE'S house from the north side, saw the pickup parked alongside a cross street, not far away. He couldn't remember seeing it there before late afternoon. A visitor, maybe?

Except that battered, beaten, rusty, nearly ancient truck looked seriously out of place in this general neighborhood.

Then he saw what appeared to be two moving heads in the darkness inside, highlighted by the brightness of the snow all around.

He tensed. Two of them. This might be it.

But he couldn't just pull two guys out of a truck. He had to catch them in the act. He couldn't even call the sheriff to watch the truck. Not now. Not when he might be overheard.

He just had to hope the loose stakeout had noticed it. And ratchet himself into serious combat mode.

ARTIE PACED THE inside of the house, ready to crawl out of her skin. *Let it be tonight*, she thought. *Just get it over.*

While there was no way to be certain that this guy meant business, that he wasn't simply a bully or a creep getting his jollies with the idea of scaring a cop, the possibility that he was serious couldn't be ignored. Nor did she want to ignore it.

It would be impossible not to fear for her father if this didn't get settled somehow.

She'd been shaken at first. Especially when the guy used her private landline number, but then she'd gotten truly worried. And now she didn't fear even the least little bit for herself. Now it was all about her dad.

So she paced the house quietly. One small lamp

burned on the mantel above the fireplace, which now glowed dull red and black with coals, all that was left of the earlier blaze.

Her night vision had adapted. She wondered if the guy outside would have less adaptation because of the snow.

And what about Boyd?

BOYD WORE A set of sunglasses, if you could call them that, purchased soon after snow started falling along his trek. Glasses that protected against the snow's glare. Glasses that sharpened the definition between objects.

Not as good as the infrared goggles he'd once used, goggles that would have made people stand out as red and yellow against the blue background of the snow and other cold things. He wished for IR but he had these glasses and they were good enough not to deprive him of all night vision around the snow.

He waited, not too close to Artie's or Clara's houses, but close enough that he'd see or hear anyone approach.

The waiting was familiar to him. Without truly good intelligence, waiting was the only smart thing to do. Alert, he settled in for however long it took.

Chapter Seventeen

"Okay," Willie said. "You still awake, Joe?"

"Yeah." Joe didn't notice that his speech was a little slurred by too much beer and couldn't see the way Willie rolled his eyes at him.

"Damn it," Willie said, punching Joe in the arm, "wake up. I don't need no drunk in the middle of this."

"I's okay. You don't hav'ta hit me."

"How drunk be you?"

"I ain't seein' double."

Willie cussed repeatedly. "Okay, we wait another hour til you git sober."

"Ain't doin' no such thing. Bein' an icicle ain't useful at all. Git to it."

Grumbling, Willie opened the door and winced as he was reminded how much it squealed.

"Oil," said Joe. "I done tol' you. Oil."

Willie told Joe to screw himself. When the two were outside the truck, they waited to see if anyone moved because of the noise of the truck door.

After a bit, Willie said. "We okay. Now don't be fallin' flat on your face in this damn snow."

Striding forward, Joe proved he could walk okay. Sort of. Willie stopped him by grabbing his arm. "Slow, you ass. Slow. Don't wanna git attention."

Joe didn't see what difference it made but walked slower anyway.

BOYD HAD BEEN keeping an eye on that truck from near the two houses, and there was no mistaking the screech of the truck's door when it opened.

They were coming.

He got into a crouch and watched, thinking they were either going to come to the front of the house or try the back way. No point in anything else.

Then he noticed how one of the guys was staggering a little.

Boyd grinned into the cold and the wind, his teeth showing. This might be fun, as long as those guys didn't shoot right off.

He was also pretty sure the sheriff's cordon was slowly closing in now. All Boyd wanted was the chance to get to these guys first.

His hands itched to throw a few punches.

AS THE TWO Lathrops edged around to the back of the house, things got a bit hairy. Willie kept glancing around but saw no one on the street. Good.

Then Joe stumbled against the side of the house with an audible thud.

Willie grabbed him by the arm and yanked him up, hard. "You lummox. You too drunk to walk. Stay put."

"Screw it," Joe answered in a whisper. "Anythin'

coulda hit the house. She ain't expectin' us. Besides, 'member what she did to Billy? We gonna need two of us."

Willie couldn't argue that. He'd heard about that baton from a friend closer to what had happened. He winced a bit at the thought and hoped Joe took most of it.

"Jest don't trip over your own damn feet."

Joe glared, the expression visible in the reflected light from the snow. Still, he moved more cautiously. He wanted this done tonight, git it over with, and not have to go runnin' like damn fools without gittin' to that woman. He patted the pistol in his belt.

Stupid place to carry a pistol, his dad had once said. *Likely to shoot off your own balls.* So Joe kept it to the side. Mostly.

INSIDE THE HOUSE, Artie heard the thud against the exterior wall. No mistaking it for a branch. No mistaking it at all. He was coming around to the back.

She snapped her baton open and took up station between the fridge and the mudroom door.

Holding that baton again made her feel a little queasy, but no way was she going to allow this guy to hurt anyone. Not anyone. Ready, she waited.

BOYD HAD MOVED in closer once he saw the direction the two men were taking. Fools, maybe, to think they'd be safer coming in the back way.

But Boyd was ready, crouched behind a shrub. Nor

did those two men appear to have any situational awareness, any idea that anyone could be watching them.

Oh, he liked the way this was going, as long as he could get to them before they got to Artie.

Then he watched them struggle with the back latch. Artie would hear it. What were these guys anyway? Stooges? Keystone Kops?

ARTIE HEARD THE back latch being fumbled. She tensed, ready to spring. Sure that Boyd couldn't be far away. Sure that this time she wasn't alone.

Then the inner door opened and she caught sight of a gun barrel. Like that? He was coming in ready to shoot anything that moved? Her stomach tightened because he might have shot her father.

Without further thought, she swung her baton and brought it down hard on the guy's forearm. He howled and the pistol skittered across the floor. She moved in, ready to strike again, when there was an explosion of activity in the mudroom.

The next thing she saw was Boyd wrestling with yet another man. *Two?* There were two?

She raised her baton, ready to help, but Boyd preempted her. A couple of punches sounded with resounding thuds and a moment later two guys were lying on the floor, one seeming unconscious, the other writhing in pain.

Boyd looked up. "Got 'em," was all he said.

THE REST OF the night turned into a kind of coffee klatch. The miscreants were carted off to the hospital in cuffs, short statements were given by both Artie and Boyd, then the rest of the surveillance team hung around for pots of coffee and some shared laughter when Boyd described what he'd seen.

"There ought to be a law against stupidity," Gage Dalton remarked, having claimed the nearest chair. He hadn't been five minutes behind his deputies. "Of course, it makes our job easier."

Eventually he rose. "We'll need official statements at the office in the morning, assuming anyone can get there."

With his departure, the group moved on.

Boyd rebuilt the fire into a pleasant blaze, and they sat silently for a long while.

"What's next?" Artie asked finally. "You're going to Seattle?"

"Yes. As soon as the storm makes flying out of here possible."

She nodded, feeling the worst ache in her heart, knowing she had no right to feel it. "I hope it all goes well with Linda."

"I think it will," he said positively, although there was a hint, just a hint, of uncertainty.

"That girl has a father to be proud of."

"One who wasn't around damn near enough." He passed a hand over his face. "Should I go rescue Clara and Herman?"

"All the police activity out here probably said enough, but you're right, I should call."

"Especially since an ambulance went out of here."

She hadn't thought of that and guilt swamped her.

Immediately, she reached for her cell and tapped in her dad's number.

Herman answered groggily, "It's okay?"

"Very okay, Dad. I'm absolutely fine, we got the bad guys."

"Good. Good. And Boyd?"

She glanced over. "I think he might have a few skinned knuckles from some punches."

Herman laughed. "I do like that boy. Tell him I'll see him in the morning. Love you, girl."

Then, as easily as slipping into a comfortable bed, Boyd and Artie slid to the floor in front of the fire.

Their lovemaking was hot, fast, ravenous. So little time left, Artie thought. So very little.

BUT THE STORM blew through the next day and Boyd packed his duffel to head to the airport.

"I'll drive you," Artie offered.

He shook his head. "I hate goodbyes, Artie."

At the door he paused and turned toward her. "Can't say when, but I'll be back, Artemis Jackson."

She nodded, managing a smile, and watched him stride out of her life just as he had hiked into it.

All she could hope was that he found the closure he so needed with his daughter. The closure that had set him out on a cross-country trek.

The trek that had wound up tearing her heart nearly in two.

He left desolation in his wake.

Chapter Eighteen

Nearly three months later, Artie had settled back into her routine as a cop. Counseling had helped her deal with the entire Lauer incident and she at last felt mostly free of it.

And with difficulty, she had begun to push Boyd Connor from her mind, if not her heart. Some things just weren't meant to be.

The sense of loss and sorrow began to ease a bit, and she started to feel comfortable in her own skin again. Some you won, some you lost.

It hadn't been meant to be. Get used to it.

But then came the twilight when she returned home in her official vehicle and saw a man sitting on her front porch step. Was that...?

Her heart flipped and nearly stopped. The man rose and there was no mistaking his figure. Boyd. God, it was Boyd!

Her hands started to shake as she wheeled her official vehicle into the driveway. She was almost scared to move. Why had he come back? To tell her in a gentlemanly way that it had been nice but he was returning to his old life? Or only because he had promised to?

Because he hadn't phoned her once in all this time and it had felt as if he dropped off the map.

But here he was. Nearly holding her breath, she switched off her ignition, opened the door and stepped out into crusty snow. He stood on the porch, waiting as she walked slowly toward him. A magnificent man in an unzipped parka, a watch cap over his dark hair. A face, strong, stern and kind all at once. A face that she cherished more than he could possibly know.

"Hi," he said quietly.

"Hi."

"I guess Herman's not here."

"Uh, he and Clara have something going on at the senior center. You been sitting in the cold for long?"

"About an hour. No big deal."

As she reached him, she thought she saw a deep warmth in his gaze.

He spoke again. "Can I hit you up for some coffee?"

"Sure," she answered, finding a bit of briskness for her voice. "You can tell me all about your daughter and how it went." And this would be as far as it went. Steeling herself, she stepped inside with him.

They settled at the kitchen table after Boyd dumped his jacket and backpack. Artie didn't want to go into the living room. It was now too full of memories she was reluctant to resurrect.

Sitting there in her uniform, she felt an unwanted distance between them. Separate paths into separate futures.

"How'd it go with Linda?" she prompted again.

One corner of his mouth lifted in smile. "Now that was interesting. Very interesting."

"How so?"

"Well, we're in family therapy right now. I had to wait for permission to leave town briefly to come see you. But that wasn't what was most interesting."

She nodded, waiting.

"I had meetings with just Linda and me with the psychologist. And that's what blew me away."

"How so?" She leaned forward a bit.

"Linda's mad at her mother now."

Artie's eyes widened. "Tell me."

Boyd shook his head. "It seems, as the full story came out, that Linda understood why the Army took me away so much. She wasn't happy about it, but she didn't blame me for it, unlike Shelley. But Linda got furious when she learned her mother had been lying to her about seeing me. It seems Shelley gave Linda the idea that I didn't want to see her. That I didn't care."

Artie drew a deep breath. "Oh, my God," she murmured. "Oh, my God."

"My reaction was a little stronger, to say the least. And Linda's was even more powerful. We're going to need some more therapy, Linda and me, but we've passed the critical point. However..." He paused. "However, it makes me sad as hell that Linda feels she can no longer trust her mother."

"That's awful!" Artie ached for a young girl who now had to feel that way about her mother, couldn't help wondering how Linda was going to learn to deal with it. Loss of trust was a *huge* thing.

"I think so, too. The psychologist isn't sure how she can mend the rift, but she wants to try. So do I, for Linda's sake."

Artie nodded, aching for him and the young woman she'd never met. "You're an awfully generous man, Boyd."

She rose and went to get more coffee, topping their mugs. "So you'll be settling in Seattle?"

"Not exactly." He stood up and began pacing the small confines of the kitchen. "I'm probably going to make a hash of all this," he said. "Be patient, please."

"Sure." At least she hoped she could. The idea of Boyd living in Seattle broke her heart wide open again. Would this sense of loss be with her forever?

"Here's the thing," Boyd said presently. "Linda has decided she wants to live with me. The psychologist wants a few more weeks to be sure Linda is really satisfied with that. I get it. But..." Then, "Ah, hell, you'll probably take this all wrong, but I don't mean it that way."

Artie leaned back, watching him with the tiniest flicker of hope and a bigger dollop of fear.

"Legally it's Linda's choice which parent she wants to live with. And she can live with me if I have a permanent domicile."

"Makes sense."

"Perfect sense. Thing is, oh, hell, Artie, I want to make my home with *you*. I've had more than three months to think about how I've been missing you, how I care about you. I won't be happy living without you. It's what I want more than damn near anything."

He paused again, sitting, facing her directly, holding her gaze with his own.

"I love you, Artie. No ifs, ands or buts. I love everything about you. But I come with a string attached, a sixteen-year-old daughter, and I'd understand perfectly if…"

Artie's heart leaped into her throat as unmitigated joy filled her. Only with effort did she restrain herself enough to say, "Linda has something to say about that."

"Yeah, but I already told her about you and this town. She's eager. We don't have to take a permanent step until you're both sure. It's just… Artie, say yes. Say you'll try."

She could barely breathe. Hope and joy overwhelmed her. "Boyd?" she whispered, hardly daring to risk all that he was suggesting.

"Yeah?"

"I have a string, too."

His face sagged a bit. "What?"

"My job. I won't quit it. I love it too much." A fact that she had at last learned about herself again.

At that his face broke into the widest smile she'd ever seen on it, making him a million times more attractive than ever to her.

"Say it, Artie. I'd never change you. Just say it, please."

"I'll try." She held her breath, trembling on the edge of a precipice as she sought to say what she had never before said. Then the words burst from her. "And what's more, Boyd Connor, I love you with every breath in my body."

Somehow they became tangled together in a blanket on the sofa, hugging so tightly it was almost bruising, kissing so deeply they stopped only to breathe.

"The three of us are going to work together," Boyd said roughly. "It's going to work. It has to."

"It will," Artie answered with utter conviction. "It will. Just don't expect me to be Linda's mother."

His head pulled back a tiny bit. "Meaning?"

"She's too old and I'm too young for that kind of relationship. So friends, okay?"

A quiet chuckle escaped him. "From what I've seen of Linda, I think she'd prefer that, too."

Then Artie laughed, the most joyous laugh that had escaped her in a while. "It'll work," she said again. "It'll work."

Because the most important part was love, and there was already plenty within her to give.

* * * * *

#2187 COLD CASE KIDNAPPING
Hudson Sibling Solutions • by Nicole Helm

Determined to find her missing sister, Dahlia Easton hires Wyoming's respected firm Hudson Sibling Solutions—and lead investigator Grant Hudson. But when Dahlia becomes the kidnapper's next target, Grant will risk everything to protect the vulnerable librarian from a dangerous cult.

#2188 UNSOLVED BAYOU MURDER
The Swamp Slayings • by Carla Cassidy

Beau Boudreau spent fifteen years paying for a murder he didn't commit. Now a free man, he recruits his ex, attorney Peyton LaCroix, to clear his name once and for all. But as their desire resurfaces, so does the killer—who wants Peyton dead...

#2189 THE SECRET OF SHUTTER LAKE
by Amanda Stevens

Abby Dallas always believed her mother abandoned her. But when investigator Wade Easton discovers skeletal remains in a car at the bottom of Shutter Lake, she learns her mother was killed...possibly by someone she knows. And Wade's protection is her only chance at survival.

#2190 POINT OF DISAPPEARANCE
A Discovery Bay Novel • by Carol Ericson

Could a recently discovered body belong to Tate Mitchell's missing childhood friend? FBI special agent Blanca Lopez thinks so—and believes the cold case is linked to another. Accessing the forest ranger's buried memories could not only solve the mystery but bring them together.

#2191 UNDER THE COVER OF DARKNESS
West Investigations • by K.D. Richards

Attorney Brandon West's client is dead, and Detective Yara Thomas suspects foul play. Working together to solve the crime exposes them to undeniable attraction...and the attention of ruthless drug dealers who will do anything, even kill, to keep their dark secrets...

#2192 SHARP EVIDENCE
Kansas City Crime Lab • by Julie Miller

Discovering a bloody knife from two unsolved murders reunites theater professor Reese Atkinson with criminalist Jackson Dobbs. The shy boy from childhood has grown into a towering man determined to keep her safe. But will it be enough to neutralize the threat?

Get 3 FREE REWARDS!

We'll send you 2 FREE Books plus a FREE Mystery Gift.

FREE
Value Over
$20

Both the **Harlequin Intrigue®** and **Harlequin® Romantic Suspense** series feature compelling novels filled with heart-racing action-packed romance that will keep you on the edge of your seat.

HARLEQUIN
PLUS

Try the best multimedia subscription service for romance readers like you!

Read, Watch and Play.

Experience the easiest way to get the romance content you crave.

Start your **FREE TRIAL** at
www.harlequinplus.com/freetrial.